THE HAVENS RAID

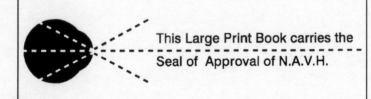

This Large Print Book carries the
Seal of Approval of N.A.V.H.

A RIDGE PARKMAN WESTERN

THE HAVENS RAID

GREG HUNT

THORNDIKE PRESS
A part of Gale, Cengage Learning

GALE
CENGAGE Learning·

Farmington Hills, Mich • San Francisco • New York • Waterville, Maine
Meriden, Conn • Mason, Ohio • Chicago

GALE
CENGAGE Learning·

Copyright © 1980 by Greg Hunt.
A Ridge Parkman Western.
Thorndike Press, a part of Gale, Cengage Learning.

LIBRARY OF CONGRESS CATALOGING-IN-PUBLICATION DATA

Names: Hunt, Greg, 1947– author.
Title: The havens raid / by Greg Hunt.
Description: Waterville, Maine : Thorndike Press, 2016. | Series: Thorndike Press
    large print western | Series: A Ridge Parkman western
Identifiers: LCCN 2016040065| ISBN 9781410489692 (hardcover) | ISBN 1410489698
    (hardcover)
Subjects: LCSH: Large type books. | GSAFD: Western stories.
Classification: LCC PS3558.U46768 H38 2016 | DDC 813/.54—dc23
LC record available at https://lccn.loc.gov/2016040065

Published in 2016 by arrangement with Greg Hunt

Printed in Mexico
1 2 3 4 5 6 7 20 19 18 17 16

THE HAVENS RAID

CHAPTER ONE

The faint trail descended the steep mountainside in a series of switchbacks, skirting treacherous outcroppings of rock and sometimes rising back up a short distance before starting down again. No trees grew on this sharply sloping side of the mountain. There was no soil adequate for anything but the most tenacious scrub brush and cactus.

Bloody Britches Trail was an ancient, seldom-used pathway and a man about had to know how it ran before he had any chance of navigating it from the ridges above to the valley below. The trail was older than anybody's recollection or any local legend. Before white men came here and put their rustic name on it, Indian hunters and war parties used it as a short cut from the valley below to the hidden draws and meadows above. But most of the Indians were gone from this region now, and the trail was only rarely ridden by a few hardy types, usually men who were on the run from somebody or those who were chasing them. But the only other way up or down this mountainside was by way of a 12-mile detour south through Last Stand Pass.

Nice names they had for landmarks in this part of the country — Last Stand Pass, Slit Throat Creek, Sniper's Rock. The names said a lot about what kind of territory it was.

Ridge Parkman knew of the Bloody Britches Trail because he had ridden through this part of the Rockies a couple of years before with a cavalry patrol in pursuit of a raiding party of renegade Apaches. The Indians had swooped in on a remote mining tent town and killed practically every man in it, and the soldiers had been dispatched from the garrison in Adobe City to capture them. They spent nine days out in these rugged mountains that time, following the false trails the Indians laid down and exhausting their supplies before finally giving up and heading back north to Adobe City without a single captive.

But this trip was different. He had come from the east this time, trailing a two-bit gunslinger named Bill Deston over 150 miles of the worst terrain these mountains could throw at a man. A week earlier Deston had robbed the small express office in Three Pines, killing the company agent and a bystander who tried to stop him. Parkman, passing through the little backwater town half a day later on his way back to Denver, learned of the robbery and took up the chase.

It was two days before Deston discovered that the deputy marshal was on his trail, but when he did find it out, he plunged into the tall timber, making a beeline toward the safety of The Havens, an outlaw stronghold deep in the rugged mountains.

But he did not make it.

His body lay now in a shallow grave up in the high country because of one fatal mistake. In this tough wild country that was all the mistakes a man was allowed sometimes.

Deston had planned his ambush well and could have knocked Parkman stone dead out of the saddle without warning, but he got jumpy and did not wait for the law man to get close enough for a sure kill. Deston's bullet had whanged off a rock behind Parkman and went singing away harmlessly, and Parkman's bullet smashed into the left side of Deston's forehead.

It was not really the way Ridge Parkman liked a chase to end. He much preferred the bother of taking a captive in to the ease of digging a grave. But when two men had to tangle out in the wilderness like this, it became a pure matter of survival and generally somebody died violently.

When Parkman searched the outlaw's gear, he found that Deston still had all the money he had taken from the freight office robbery, the entire $84. That was $28 for each life he had destroyed, including his own. He also found a letter on him from his mother asking when he would give up this roaming around and come home to run the family farm in Iowa.

The chase had taken its toll on Parkman. To catch the outlaw he had to ride longer hours than his prey, gnawing meals of tough jerky and hardtack in the saddle and grabbing only brief hours of sleep with one eye always open. After he buried Deston he made a proper camp with boiled coffee, fried bacon and beans, and a night of peaceful sleep, but he was still haggard and exhausted. He had burned away several pounds during the chase and his belt was one notch tighter than when he left Three Pines.

When Deston was planted, instead of turning around and heading back the way he had come, he decided to ride the shorter distance on into Adobe City. Henry Lott ran the U.S. Marshal's office there and he could send word to Denver that Ridge would be headed on in after a few days of rest.

But at the moment his thoughts dwelled mainly on just riding President Grant down from the treacherous mountain slopes to the wide green valley below. He looked forward to the easy riding there, as well as to bedding down beside a cool stream and turning his horse loose to graze in the lush green grass of the valley floor.

Finally he wound his way around the last tangled mass of boulders and he was down from the slope. The trail ended there. Ridge rode across a few rolling foothills and then out onto the flat valley floor. The sun was just dropping below the horizon with a big show of bright reds, oranges, and pinks in the western sky when he spotted a small grove of trees ahead in the distance and decided to make his camp there for the night.

It was President Grant who gave the first warning that everything was not as peaceful as it seemed in the trees ahead. When they were still over 100 yards away, the horse began to snort nervously and show signs that he was not too happy about something. Parkman drew his Colt revolver and slowed the mount to an easy walk. President Grant was normally not a skittish animal, but he did have a keen sense of danger which had more than once kept Ridge from riding unaware into a nest of trouble.

Parkman considered just skirting the grove and riding on, but his curiosity and some logical thinking kept him from doing that. If there was some sort of danger there, it would probably be better to go ahead and deal with it than to go on down the trail not knowing what sort of threat might be dogging him.

When they were within about 30 yards of the trees, the scent began to invade Ridge's nostrils. It was the ripe, ugly odor of death. As they drew closer, the smell became oppressive and sickening. At the edge of the grove, Ridge halted the horse and spent a moment just examining the area ahead closely before going on.

The grove of cottonwoods and aspens was only about 50 feet across. A small stream trickled down its middle and there was a little clearing which had been used recently by somebody as a campsite. But still he could not see what dead thing was putting out the awful smell. He moved forward cautiously toward the clearing, now having to urge his horse to continue in that direction as he calmed the animal with quiet re-assurances. He stopped in the clearing and stepped easily to the ground.

Then he saw the boots. They were hanging down through the lower branches of a tree about 10 feet away and spun slightly as a capricious breeze disturbed them. Parkman holstered his revolver and walked around until he could see the entire body of the man who hung there.

The dead man wore plain cowboy clothes, denim trousers, cotton shirt, and leather vest. His hands and feet were tied with short strips of lariat. The rope that held him aloft was slung over a high branch and then brought down and tied to a lower one. Atop an unnaturally long, twisted neck, the head gazed down at Ridge, blue-black, fat tongue protruding from a gaping mouth, bulging eyes seeming to stare at him with fixed disinterest.

Ridge untied the end of the rope and lowered the dead man's body to the ground. It was then that he first saw the shiny star pinned to his shirt beneath the vest. It was a deputy U.S. Marshal's badge. Ridge stepped forward and kneeled beside the body, studying the facial features closely and trying to imagine how they had looked before the devastating contortions of death and decay took over.

He knew the man. His name was Mark Franklin and he had worked out of the Adobe City office under the direction of Henry Lott. He and Ridge had seldom worked together, but they were friends and Ridge knew his reputation was that of a dedicated and capable law man. From the state of his body, he had probably been hanging there three or four days.

Staring down at Franklin's body, a seething anger began to rise in Parkman toward whoever had chosen this particularly humiliating way to execute a fellow deputy marshal. It was one thing for a law man to die in a shootout — that was a possibility they all faced — but Franklin had obviously been taken captive and there was no sense in killing him this way.

"We'll get the bastards that did this, Franklin," Parkman promised the corpse. He was normally not an overly vengeful man, but this kind of killing brought out a cold, ruthless determination in him.

The light was almost gone now, but Ridge still scouted around the grove for some signs of what had gone on here. A shower a day or two before had obliterated most of the signs, but he did find a place where a few horses had been hobbled for a while. He checked the edge of the grove for some indication of which way the men had ridden out, but in the quickly approaching darkness he could find nothing.

Returning to the clearing, Ridge unsaddled President Grant, watered him at the stream, and then led him to the edge of the grove where there was plenty of grass for him to graze on. He knew the loyal animal would not roam out of whistling distance before morning.

Next came the unpleasant job of taking care of Mark Franklin's body. Ridge unpinned the badge from his shirt, then went through his pockets and removed his scant personal belongings. There was not much, just a pocket knife, a small locket with the picture of a young woman in it, a battered pipe, a cloth bag full of tobacco, and a worn deck of cards. His gunbelt and whatever money he may have had were apparently taken by whoever killed him.

It was hard for Ridge to dig a decent grave for Franklin because he had no shovel and the only tool he had which was even halfway suitable for digging was his long sheath knife. To get Deston in the ground Ridge had merely scooped out a shallow trench with a sharp rock, put the body in it, and covered it over with big rocks, but he was determined to give his fellow deputy a proper resting place. It was little enough to do for a good man who had bought it this way.

He chose a shaded spot not far from the stream and set to work, loosening up the soft dirt with the knife blade and raking it out with his hands. Though exhausted even before he started, he worked on the grave late into the night, pausing only occasionally to get a drink from the stream before going back to work. The moon had risen midway in the sky before he finished the hole. It was two feet wide, a little over six feet long and four feet deep.

Returning to where Franklin's body lay, Ridge spread his slicker out on the ground and rolled the body over onto it. Then he dragged the slicker over to the grave. He wrapped the dead marshal in the slicker and bound it securely, then used his lariat to lower the body into the grave. It took a long time to fill the grave in because Ridge worked carefully, packing the dirt as best he could and mounding the top up neatly.

Next he cut two sticks off a nearby tree and fashioned a cross, notching the two pieces so they fit together tightly and then securing them with some horseshoe nails he carried. Finally he nailed Franklin's badge to the center of the cross and hammered the sharpened end of the cross into the ground at the head of the grave.

When the chore was finished, he stood up and stared grimly down at his work. "Well, Franklin," he said, "this is one helluva way for a man like you that could shoot straight and fight hard and knew right from wrong to end up, but you chose the life and you knew the risks. Ain't nobody ever promised none of us that we'd live to bounce our grandbabies on our knees an' tell 'em stories about how it was.

"I'm mighty sorry I can't even leave your name marked here, but if anybody comes along an' finds this grave, they'll see that star an' they'll know one good man is layin' underneath it. *Vaya con Dios,* my friend."

The new day was just beginning to inch its way over the ragged peaks to the east. Parkman got the bedroll off the back of his saddle and plopped down tiredly, bothering only to pull off his boots before allowing sleep to come at last.

CHAPTER TWO

Adobe City, like most of the other towns and cities in this part of Colorado, had begun its existence as a gathering place where miners could buy supplies, drink whiskey, chase whores, and kill each other with regularity. At first there was no plan to its growth. Men simply built where they found a vacant spot of ground, streets took off in their own meandering directions, and businesses were opened up haphazardly on any available land near the center of town.

But Adobe City, unlike many other mining towns in the mountains, had two things going for it. It was the center of a lucrative mining area which continued to produce after others had failed, and it straddled a major transportation route which crossed the mountains from Denver. Eventually men with foresight and grand dreams began to form a local government to bring some order out of the chaos which ruled there.

That was several years before, and the rapid growth had continued. Now Adobe City could boast a permanent population of nearly 4,000, a three-story brick courthouse, federal building and jail, and upwards of 200 businesses, including twenty-three saloons, two banks, four hotels, six brothels, a Wells Fargo terminal, and just about every other kind of business which might be found in any other large city farther to the east. A large and constantly expanding warehouse district dominated the center of town in a long strip along the railroad tracks, and was quickly becoming the center of local commerce and wealth.

By the time Ridge Parkman rode President Grant into the outskirts of Adobe City two days after burying Mark Franklin, he was about to fall out of the saddle from exhaustion, and the big strong horse was also badly in need of a long rest. He cast a longing look at every saloon he rode by, thinking how good a cold beer would taste at that moment, and he heaved an audible sigh as he passed the Bridger Hotel. But he could not stop anywhere along the street. He would soon get his chance for refreshment and rest, but other matters were more important and had to be taken care of first.

When he reached a stable near the courthouse, he stepped to the ground and turned the reins over to a boy who came running out to meet him. As he pulled his rifle out of the saddle boot and untied his saddle-bags, he told the towheaded youth, "Plenty of grain, not too much water at first, an' rub him down like he was your own. You take good care of my friend here, an' I'll take good care of you. Okay, *amigo*?"

"Sure, mister. He's gonna think he's done died an' gone to horse heaven, I'll treat him so fine. You a marshal?"

" 'Fraid so."

"Where'd you ride in from?"

Ridge raised his rifle and pointed south toward the wild country.

"You chase an outlaw into The Havens?"

"I chased an outlaw, but he didn't make it into The Havens, boy, nor heaven either, prob'ly." To cut the questioning short, he turned and started down the street toward the courthouse.

The offices used by the U.S. Marshals were on the second floor near the back of the large brick courthouse. As was his custom, Ridge entered the building by the back door and went up a small rear staircase to the second floor. He never entered this building by the front door, preferring to keep his visits here as unobtrusive and unnoticed as possible. That was a quirk of his, like not wearing his badge except when it was necessary. Generally, he figured, the fewer people who knew he was a deputy marshal the better, and when he wanted somebody to know it, he told them.

He entered the empty outer office without knocking. Captain Henry Lott, the head marshal there, was allowed money in his budget for a secretary and clerk, but he preferred to use the appropriations to put another marshal in the field and he did his own filing and paperwork. Ridge stuck his head through the doorway to the inner office and said, "Hey, Henry? You receivin' visitors?"

Lott had risen from his desk when he heard the cuter door open and close, and now he came to meet Ridge with an outstretched hand. "Ridge Parkman!" he exclaimed. "You mean to tell me they're still lettin' you carry a gun an' call yourself a law man?"

"They ain't found me out yet, I reckon," Ridge drawled, shaking the older man's hand warmly. Since he last saw Lott several months before, it seemed that he was a touch grayer at the temples and had a few new wrinkles on his weathered face, but he still stood ramrod straight, a towering figure at six foot two. At fifty-four, his powerful body was still in better shape than that of most men half his age.

Ridge dropped his saddlebags on the floor and leaned his rifle against a chair. "I'm bringin' bad news, Henry," he said. "I found Mark Franklin 'bout forty miles south, of here, strung up in a tree an' dead as hell."

Lott's eyes narrowed and the firm features of his face turned to stone as anger and sadness mingled there. "Damn those sonsofbitches!" he stormed, crashing his fist on the desk in frustration. "Damn 'em!"

"You know who might of done it?" Ridge asked. "I'd sure love to get 'em in my gun sights for about ten seconds."

"It had to be some of Blackie Crystal's bunch," Lott said. "That's who Franklin an' Billy Dean Holley were after last time I saw 'em six days ago."

"I've heard of Crystal," Ridge allowed, "but this is the first time I ever heard of him strayin' up this far north. I thought his specialty was raidin' the towns down along the Mexican border in Texas."

"It was 'til the Texas Rangers got fed up with it an' tied into him. Accordin' to the word I got, the Rangers got special authorization from the Mexican Government an' dogged Blackie an' his bunch nearly sixty miles into Mexico before they forced a showdown. Killed somethin' like twenty of 'em, but Blackie an' about ten others got away . . . jus' disappeared.

"We'd heard rumors that they might be up this way hidin' out in The Havens, but nobody knew for sure what become of 'em until eight days ago when they blasted their way into a bank here in town an' got away with fourteen thousand dollars. Killed two guards an' a clerk in the bank, an' then gunned two city policemen once they got outside. It was a real bloodbath. There was twelve of 'em, includin' Blackie.

"We got up a posse of about twenty-five men an' lit out after 'em, but they jus' kept splittin' up an' splittin' up until it was hard to tell who was goin' where. Slick as hell the way they did it, makin' us divide our group until most of the townsmen were in such small bunches that they got scared an' come on back to town."

As he told Ridge of the chase, Lott got a bottle of bourbon and two glasses from a cabinet and poured drinks for Ridge and himself, then motioned Ridge to a chair in front of the desk. Then the head marshal sat down in the swivel chair behind the desk.

"Finally," he continued, "there wasn't but just me an' my two men, Franklin an' Holley, an' two city policemen left out there. Franklin an' Holley took out after two men an' I led the police after three more. We caught up with the bastards we was followin' an' they turned out to be Blackie Crystal, Mexican Joe Rodriguez, an' Sam Platshaw. We killed Sam an' brought Blackie an' the Mexican back. We got 'em here in the jail now waitin' for trial.

"But Franklin an' Holley never came back. We never got any word from them 'til today, an' that wasn't good news."

"Wal, at least you got their head honcho," Ridge said. "When you get him shipped off to hell it won't be near as hard to take care of the rest of them."

"I thought the same thing 'til this morning," Lott said. "Then this came to me in the mail." He pushed an envelope across the desk for Ridge to inspect. Inside was a note and a Masonic ring with the initials "BDH" inscribed behind the set. Ridge unfolded the note and read the message there, scratched on the paper in crude penciled printing. It said: WE GOT THE MAN THAT WOR THIS RING AN WE KIL HIM IF YOU DONT TURN BLACKEE AN JO LOOS!

"Nice fellers. Guess they figgered they didn't need two hostages so they just hung one up in a tree to get him out of their hair."

24

"Yeah. Poor Franklin," Lott said quietly. "Damn good man."

"Yeah, I hate that," Ridge agreed. "I buried him the best I could an' I brought his stuff along in case he's got family." He reached in his saddlebags and got out Franklin's few possessions wrapped in a bandanna. "Ain't much," he said.

"I'll take 'em to his wife," Lott said. "She runs a small shop here in town. She was always tryin' to get Mark to quit an' become a shopkeeper, but he wouldn't. He had a lot of dedication to this work." The captain paused and picked up first Franklin's pipe and then the locket he had carried with his wife's picture in it. "This is the worst part of my job," he continued at last, "telling families that their men are dead."

"I'm glad I don't have to do it, cap'n. But at least he died for the right reasons. Not like that other feller I left in a grave out there. Bill Deston."

"Deston? I think I have a flier on him here someplace. Claim jumpin' or somethin'. What'd you nail him for?"

"He stuck up the freight office in Three Pines an' gunned down a couple of men." Ridge got a second bundle with Deston's things in it and passed it over to Lott. "His gear wasn't no count so I just left it out

25

there an' turned his horse loose. It looked like it needed a little freedom after the hard life Deston give it. Was there any bounty on his head?"

"Hell, Parkman, you know I couldn't pay you bounty for doin' your job," Lott growled.

"I wasn't thinkin' that, Henry," Ridge told him. "There's a letter from his mother in there an' it seems like she's run into some hard times. I was jus' thinkin' . . ."

"Send her the money an' tell her it was his?"

"She didn't know he was a bandit, I reckon. Seems to me it wouldn't hurt for her to think her son made somethin' of himself before he died."

"I'll think on it," Lott promised.

They talked on for the length of time it took to drink another glass of Lott's mellow bourbon, bringing each other up to date on the happenings on either side of the range of mountains. But finally Ridge decided that he had to bring the conversation to a close and find himself a bed before he collapsed from exhaustion. "Cap'n, I'm goin' to have to find the nearest hotel an' see if I can't talk 'em into lettin' me use one of their beds," Ridge said, " 'fore I pass out right here in the middle of your office."

"Sure, go ahead, Ridge," Lott said. "You look plumb awful. Even worse than usual." A slight smile appeared under his bushy, salt-and-pepper panhandle mustache.

"If it wasn't one of my rules to be kind to old codgers," Ridge grinned tiredly, "I might tend to take that personal an' put a big knot on that ol' gray head of yours."

He was about to leave when the outer office door opened and a young woman walked in. She looked Ridge up and down, taking in at a glance his dirty, sweat-stained clothing and his unshaven face. "Is Captain Lott in?" she asked.

"Why yes, ma'am, he is," Ridge said from the doorway of Lott's office. "He's right here." She returned his smile halfheartedly, but it faded quickly from her face. She was careful not to brush against his dirty clothing as she passed through the doorway into the inner office.

She was about twenty-five, with shimmering black hair and a face pretty enough to stop a man still in his tracks. Under the simple white dress she wore was a figure as fetching as a handful of double eagles.

"Morning, Rosalie," Lott said without much enthusiasm. He did not seem particularly happy about her showing up here in his office.

"Captain, I just came by to check . . ." she began, but Lott interrupted her.

"Rosalie, I'd like for you to meet somebody," he told her. "Rosalie Holley, this is Ridge Parkman, another of our marshals from over on the Denver side."

"Oh, yes. I've heard Billy Dean speak of you," she told Ridge. "I'm happy to meet you." There seemed to be a little less coolness in her attitude now that she knew he was a law man.

"Me too, ma'am," Ridge said. "You'll have to excuse the way I look right now. I've been in the saddle for nigh onto a week an' a half now, an' I know I must smell like the dead bull in the barnyard. Are you Billy Dean's missus?"

"I'm his sister," Rosalie told him. "And please don't worry about your appearance. I know what kind of hard job you have to do and I understand." Turning back to Lott, she said, "I wanted to check and see if there's been any word about my brother."

Ridge glanced at the captain, not envying him his task right now. He was curious about how Lott would handle the situation, whether he would tell the girl everything or choose to leave her in the dark about her brother's situation.

The captain was direct and bluntly truthful with the girl. "I just got a message this morning," Lott said quietly. "He's alive, but I'm afraid it don't look good." He handed her the envelope with the ring and the note in it.

She gazed at the message a moment and then looked up at Lott. "Well, you're going to let him go, aren't you? This Blackie whoever they want?"

There was deep concern in the captain's eyes as he returned the girl's stare. "No, Rosalie," he said. "I'm afraid not. We can't."

"But they have my brother!" she insisted, her voice rising as she neared hysteria. "They'll kill Billy if you don't do what they ask!"

"But if we let Blackie Crystal go, there's no telling how many more people he might kill before somebody gets him again. This is just the kind of demand that the United States Marshals can't give in to. If we did, there'd be hostages being snatched up everywhere to use as barter for jailed criminals."

"Captain, you have to!" the girl insisted, throwing the note down on the desk and bursting into tears. "Billy's your friend. You can't just let him die!"

"We don't aim to," Lott said. "We'll do all we can to get him back alive, but if it was my own mother they had out there, I wouldn't open that cell door for Blackie Crystal and that Mexican. They're that bad."

Rosalie Holley looked up at Ridge through reddened eyes, seeming to implore him to side with her. He knew he should do something, to say a few words of consolation at least, but no words came. He stood there awkwardly, feeling like the boy that dropped the baby.

"Ridge works out of the Denver office, but I'm keeping him here to work on this case," Lott said. That pronouncement surprised Ridge because there had been no mention of it earlier. He guessed that it might have been a spur of the moment decision by Lott, but he was glad. Ridge wanted to get his hands on Mark Franklin's killers. "And I'm callin' in every available marshal in the state," the captain continued. "That scum out there in The Havens is goin' to have hell to pay for killin' one of my men an' holding another one for hostage."

"Killing?" Rosalie repeated with a look of shock.

"Ridge found Mark Franklin dead out there," Lott said. Ridge was relieved that the captain did not go into the details of the death.

"Oh, dear God," Rosalie muttered. "Poor Beth. Does she know yet?"

"I'll be going over to tell her in a few minutes," Lott said.

"I'll go with you, captain. She'll need somebody with her for a while."

"That'd be fine if you'd do that, Rosalie. I'd sure be obliged."

Ridge retrieved his rifle and saddlebags. "Well, Henry, if you don't need anything else from me, I think I'll find me that bed."

"Go ahead. I'll get a message off to Denver, an' we'll talk again later after you've rested an' cleaned up."

"Sounds fine," Ridge said, tipping his hat to Rosalie Holley. He turned to start out, but she stopped him impulsively.

"Marshal Parkman, I guess it's been awhile since you had a home-cooked meal," she said. "Would you care to come to our house some night for supper? I'm sure Mother would be glad to have a friend of Billy Dean's over."

"I can't think of hardly anything I'd like better," Ridge said.

The three of them left the office together, but in the hall Lott and Rosalie started away toward the front entrance while Ridge turned to leave by the back.

CHAPTER THREE

The heavy shades were drawn over the window and little of the afternoon light from the setting sun leaked through into Ridge's hotel room. The place was filled with a comfortable, brown murkiness, as well as with the heavy odor of his own filthy body and clothes. He had been awake for about half an hour, but he had not gotten up yet. He was just lying there, smoking cigarettes and enjoying the luxury of a real mattress as he rehashed in his mind the occurrences of the last few days.

It was odd, he thought, how events sometimes buffeted a man around, jerking him off the path he thought he was following and sending him off in totally unexpected directions at a moment's notice.

Several days ago, as he rode into Three Pines on his way back to Denver, he had expected things to happen entirely different. When he got to Denver, he planned to stop by headquarters and check in, then head down to the hotel room he rented to clean up and maybe grab a few hours of sleep. Then he would go see that pretty little thing who waited tables at the Colorado House, hoping that she could be persuaded to spend the rest of the evening with him after she got off work. She was just off the boat from Germany a few months before, and apart from the restaurant terminology, her English was atrocious, but she had a quick smile and laughing dark eyes that did all the communicating a man could want.

Thinking of the girl, he didn't even plan a stop in Three Pines in his hurry to get back. But then the Bill Deston thing came up. Three Pines was too small to have any law man of its own, and though a call had gone out for the local sheriff in a neighboring town, he had never arrived. Ridge knew that if somebody didn't get on the outlaw's trail soon, it would be too late to ever catch up to him. So he had turned west and started dogging the outlaw's trail into the mountains. That turn had led him here into the midst of all this confusion and trouble.

But it was the sort of thing Parkman had become used to after so many years as a law man. Trouble always came when it was least expected. The possibility of death lurked constantly in the immediate future, and when there was danger to be faced or fighting to be done, it seemed like he always turned out to be right in the thick of it, sticking his neck out when nobody else could or would.

Because of that, he had developed a sort of temporary outlook on life. He thought about the future, about how if he was destined to have a future what he wanted it to be like, but he had also learned to make the most of the little pleasures and comforts along the way . . . like now. He was anticipating a bath with great delight. Pretty soon he would get up and go downstairs to wash up, and then he would put on the clean outfit of clothes which he had been carrying with him for nearly three weeks in anticipation of this opportunity.

And then there was Adobe City to be explored. There was a lot of fun and deviltry to be had out there for a man with a few dollars in his pocket, and he had no intention of reporting back to Henry Lott until he had spent a respectable amount of time and cash indulging himself. Maybe after he had had his bath, a full meal, several drinks, and a few more hours in the comfortable oblivion of sleep, he would feel more receptive to discussing with Lott some reckless scheme to save Billy Dean Holley's neck and get revenge on a gang of killers and thieves.

The knock at the door was so light that at first he thought someone was knocking at one of the other doors down the hall. Then the light rapping sounded again and a woman's voice said, "Ridge? Are you in there?" It was the voice of Rosalie Holley.

"Give me a minute," Ridge said as he slid his feet to the floor and reached for his pants. He had stripped down to his long-handles before climbing into bed. Once he had donned his trousers and shirt, he went to the door and unlocked it. He opened it to admit Rosalie Holley, then returned to the table along one wall and put a match to the wick of a lamp.

"Leave the door open if you like," he told Rosalie. "I don't know how you feel about being alone with a man in a hotel room."

"I think we're better off with it shut," she said, pushing the door closed without hesitation. "I don't think Captain Lott would want a lot of people to see us together here."

Ridge turned and asked with a grin, "Ol' Henry ain't goin' prudish in his old age, is he?"

"No, it's nothing like that," Rosalie said.

"It's something about a plan he has. He said he didn't want to come and see you himself, and he told me not to let anybody see us talking if I could help it."

She looked puzzled by the frown which crossed Ridge's features, but still went on with her message. "Captain Lott said he wanted some private place away from his office to talk to you, and we decided that our house might be the best place. I came to invite you over to supper tonight."

Ridge looked back at her, trying not to show the aggravation he felt. He saw the pleasant evening he had plotted shoved out the window by his duty and the impatience of the captain.

Rosalie sensed his mood and said defensively, "It's a plan to save Billy's life, Marshal. Every minute he's in the hands of those monsters decreases the chances that we'll ever see him alive again."

Ridge knew she was near tears and spoke up quickly to reassure her. "I'm ready to go the limit to get him back," he promised. "An' what with the secret meetings an' all, Henry must have himself one real humdinger of a plan."

"I hope he does," the woman told him quietly. "It's going to take something close to a miracle to get my brother out of that outlaw camp alive."

"Guess we'll just have to come up with a danged miracle, then. You know, we marshals stick together pretty close an' when some polecat bothers with one of our own, or kills one, we take it as an extra special insult to all of us. We jus' don't like to let folks get away with things like that, an' very few ever do."

"I know you'll do your best," Rosalie said. "Now about supper, how does eight o'clock suit you?"

"That's fine," Ridge told her. "I jus' need some time to scrape a few layers of dirt off an' dig some bearable clothes out of my kit."

She gave him instructions about how to find their house, then opened the door and checked the hallway before leaving.

When she was gone, Ridge got his saddlebags and pulled out his shaving gear and the change of clothes before heading downstairs to the bathroom in the back of the hotel. The water in the huge iron tub was murky from a few previous uses, but Ridge still plunged in with unrestrained pleasure. He could not remember exactly how long it had been since he had been able to take a whole bath, but he was sure it was close to a month.

After the bath he finished his grooming at

the small washbasin and mirror, dressed in his dean outfit, and left. He dropped off his dirty clothes and shaving gear in his room, left his room key at the front desk, and started off into town. It was still only a little past seven and he had some time to sample the Adobe City nightlife before he headed to the Holley home for supper.

By the time Ridge left the saloon district and started strolling his way toward the quieter residential part of town, he was feeling the pleasant glow of the three beers he had sloshed down in three separate saloons. He knew he risked offending Rosalie Holley and her mother by showing up at their home with alcohol on his breath, but he had to take his fun when he could. He well knew that at any time he might be ordered back into the saddle to spend days or weeks far from any city or town, and he did not want to spend all that time wishing he had downed a beer when he had the chance.

He walked for several blocks past the large warehouses packed tightly together near the railroad switch yards, then passed through an area of small shops and markets which catered to the needs of the railroad and warehouse laborers who lived and worked nearby.

The farther he walked from the heart of town, the better the housing conditions grew. From one end of Missouri Street, a long main thoroughfare, to the other, the homes ranged from the poorest hovels at one end, to the classiest mansions at the other. The Holley family lived somewhere in the middle. Their four-room frame house was small and simple, but it was well cared for. The house had recently been whitewashed and the small front yard was surrounded by a neat, low picket fence.

Ridge passed through the gate and walked up the stone pathway to the front porch. Rosalie must have been watching for him, because she opened the front door only a second after he knocked on it.

She looked even more beautiful tonight. She had changed into a pale blue dress of patterned material with tufted sleeves and an elaborately embroidered pattern across the bodice. She had piled and pinned her long dark hair on top of her head and, Ridge noticed with approval, had applied just the slightest touch of color to her lips.

His glance must have remained on her overly long, because at last, with a nervous smile, Rosalie said, "Good evening, Marshal. I hope I pass inspection."

" 'Scuse me," Ridge said, slightly embarrassed. "It's just that a man with a wan-derin' job like mine don't get many chances to spend time in the company of a lady like you. Guess I don't know much about how to act."

"There's nothing wrong with the way you act," Rosalie said lightly. "You act like a man, and I like that."

Henry Lott appeared in the doorway behind Rosalie and said, "Hey, Ridge. I see you found the place."

"Yeah, I came right to it."

"Good. Come on in an' I'll pour you a drink."

Ridge followed the captain and their host-ess into a small sitting room which was half filled with a dining table set for four. As Rosalie showed him to a seat, Lott went to a small side table and poured whiskey into two glasses, allaying Ridge's apprehensions about the drinks he had already had.

When Lott brought one of the glasses over to Ridge, he said, "It prob'ly seems strange to you, me wantin' to meet out here to discuss business, but I've got my reasons."

"I never doubted but what you did, Henry. I've known you too long to think you do much of anything without a good reason."

"Well, I've got a plan, Ridge. I've been busy all afternoon sending out wires and meeting with the commander of the army garrison here. I've just about . . ."

Lott was interrupted by the entrance of a woman from the kitchen. She carried two steaming dishes of food to the table, then turned to the three of them in the sitting room. As Ridge and Lott rose to their feet, Rosalie said, "Marshal Parkman, this is my mother, Maureen Holley. Mother, this is Ridge Parkman."

Somehow Ridge was prepared to meet a small, elderly woman with gray hair and eyes reddened from crying over her son, but Mrs. Holley was not at all what he had expected. She was a tall woman in her late forties. Her face had a look of determination and character which Ridge should have expected of the mother of Billy and Rosalie, and if she had been crying recently over Billy, there was no indication of it on her attractive, smiling features. She crossed the room and shook Ridge's hand warmly.

"Welcome to our home, Ridge," she said with a demure smile. "Henry has told me you will be helping out with the plan to get my son back to safety."

"Yes, ma'am," Ridge said. "At this point you prob'ly know more about it than I do, but I'm willin' to do anything I can to help him."

"You might not say that once you hear the plan," Lott mumbled over the top of his upturned glass.

Ridge glanced over at the captain with a question in his eyes, but he let his questions go unasked. He knew he would find out soon enough what the plan was, and if Henry Lott said he would not like it, chances are he would not

"It looks like dinner is ready, gentlemen," Rosalie said. "Would you like to come over and have a seat?" As Ridge and Lott found places at the table, Rosalie and her mother went in the kitchen and brought out the last of the food.

It was a delicious meal of roast beef and fresh garden vegetables, and for a few minutes everybody ate with relish. Finally, though, as plates were being helped for the second time, Lott began to discuss the ideas he had been working on.

"Ridge," he said. "I was telling Maureen and Rosalie before you came, that there is no way we could ever let Blackie Crystal and Mexican Joe out of jail like the note ordered, and I think they understand why now. We'd all lose our jobs if we did, and I really don't think it would make any difference to Billy Dean in the end. These are desperate, absolutely ruthless men an' they'd prob'ly still kill him.

"Now we could take troops out there an' charge The Havens, but Captain Hennessey an' I have talked this over an' we think it's a situation that calls more for the use of strategy than it does of sheer force an' fire power. That's where you come in."

"I'm your strategy?" Ridge asked with a grin.

"You're a key part of it. We've decided that we have to take some kind of gamble here, so we're going to let Blackie an' Joe escape from jail. But you, Ridge, are going to be our hole card — you're going to escape with them."

As Lott paused a moment for emphasis, Ridge stared across the table at him, nodding his understanding. The captain had been right a few minutes before. It was not a plan Ridge liked, but he saw the logic behind it, and he did not show any dissatisfaction by word or expression. He knew if the situation were reversed, Billy Dean Holley would accept such an assignment without hesitation to save Ridge or any other of his fellow marshals.

"We picked you for the job because you haven't worked much in this part of the state," Lott told Ridge, "an' there will be less chance that any of Crystal's bunch or anybody else out there in The Havens will recognize you."

"Makes sense."

"Yeah. That doesn't mean you definitely won't run into somebody that knows you, but you'll just have to deal with that if it happens. You're the best chance we've got on short notice."

"So pretty soon I'm going to get tossed in the lockup, an' then I'll turn around an' escape again, taking Blackie an' Mexican Joe with me."

"Something like that, but we've added a few touches to make it believable."

"I bet you have," Ridge said wryly.

Over dessert and coffee, Lott began outlining to Ridge the arrangements which had been made with the city police, the jailers at the courthouse, and the Army commander. Ridge would get his night out on the town as he had hoped, but it would not end in the most enjoyable way. About midnight he would be arrested by the city police and thrown into the jail below the courthouse.

The escape was scheduled for the early morning hours, and before that time Ridge would have to win the confidence of Blackie and Joe, and somehow make them decide to go with him.

Once they were gone, Lott would begin

planning a full-scale assault on The Havens, but that would not take place for days. For one thing, it would take him awhile to assemble the necessary force of marshals, soldiers, and volunteers, and he also wanted to give Ridge a little while to arrange the escape of Billy Dean Holley, and, if possible, to get out himself with Blackie as his prisoner.

"That's going to be the toughest part of the whole assignment," Lott explained. "To justify letting him escape, we're going to have to get him back in the end. You'll have to stay with them 'til you can do that, an' if you finally decide there's no way to get him out, well . . ." he paused and glanced anxiously at the women, ". . . if you can't get him out, you do what has to be done."

Again Ridge nodded his silent understanding, but again he did not like it. He was in a violent profession and there had been times in his life, plenty of them, when he had no choice but to kill. He had killed before, and when it was necessary, he performed the job coldly and without hesitation. But this was the first time he had ever been ordered to kill, and that order left a bad taste with him. Yet he knew it was an order that Henry Lott would not issue lightly, and he knew it was a necessity in this particular case.

Blackie Crystal was a vicious criminal, a heartless killer himself, and his life must be taken. Only Ridge Parkman would be able to decide whether it came from a bullet or a hangman's noose.

After supper, the tone in the home was subdued. Despite the brave front they were showing, the two Holley women were deeply worried about Billy Dean, and after meeting Ridge and hearing the dangerous mission he had been given, they were also concerned for his safety.

Lott stayed only long enough to be courteous, then excused himself and left to complete the final arrangements for Ridge's capture and escape. They had already agreed on what saloon Parkman could be found in at midnight, and he knew what sign would indicate that he should start to break out of the jail.

Ridge stayed around the Holley home awhile longer. He was not overly anxious to leave the company of these two pleasant and attractive women and begin his work, and he did not want to be out in the saloons too long before going to jail. When he was captured, he must appear to be drunk, but it could be suicidal to actually get drunk before beginning a job such as this.

Soon Maureen Holly got up to begin

clearing the dishes from the table, and Rosalie suggested that she and Ridge take a walk. Ridge readily agreed.

She led him down a few quiet residential streets on a route which eventually led them to the edge of town and beyond. It was a bright moonlit night and the woman's steps did not pause as they passed the last house and headed toward the wooded hills in the distance.

They were quiet for much of the walk, each thinking his own thoughts, but finally when they reached a small stream and paused, Rosalie turned, to Ridge and said, "I've been trying to figure out a way to tell you how grateful I am to you for going out after Billy Dean the way you are."

She looked at his face a moment, and then turned away slightly, her eyes wandering to the distant silhouetted mountains as she continued. "Probably you don't know this about our family, but we had another law man in the family years ago. My father. He was a city policeman in St. Louis when Billy Dean and I were just children, but he was killed thirteen years ago when he ran into a burning building to save a man. The building came down on top of them, and we found out later it was a saloonkeeper he went in after. Can you believe that? A saloonkeeper. My mother acted very brave about it, like she's acting now, but the pain she kept inside still almost killed her.

"We moved out here six years ago and mother was hoping that Billy would choose to get into some kind of business or professional job. I knew better. I knew he never had any plans except to be a law man, too.

"She didn't object when he joined the marshals. She has never tried to stop us from anything we decided to do with our lives, but I could see the old fears and pains there, locked deep inside her. It's almost like she had known all along that this day, this kind of tragedy, would come again."

Ridge could see that she was crying now, and he reached out without thinking and put his arm around her shoulders. He felt the slight trembling in her body as she continued.

"It's odd, me telling all of this to a man I only met this morning, but suddenly you've become a very important person in our lives. I just wanted you to know, you're our only hope and I know you can do it. I know you'll bring Billy back to us alive."

"I'll do it or die tryin'," Ridge promised.

"No! Don't die!" Rosalie said. "Please don't die!"

"Okay, I won't."

She turned to him, her hands lightly find-ing his shoulders and a tearful smile coming to her features. "You're teasing me now," she said. "You know what I mean, though. If Billy came back and you didn't, it would be almost as bad as if neither of you did."

"I have to agree with you there."

"Just bring him back, and bring yourself back," she said pleadingly. Suddenly she reached up and pulled his head down to hers. She kissed him with lips that were at once tender and hungry. Ridge could sense in her kiss a simple human need to be held and comforted, to be close to somebody during this confusing and upsetting time, but there was something else there, too, something he would not allow himself to identify and explore.

"If you bring him back, I promise . . ."

"Wait a minute," Ridge interrupted, eas-ing her away from him slightly so he could look down into her eyes. "I'm goin' out there to The Havens to do my job, Rosalie. I'd go after Billy even if he wasn't nobody's son or brother, so don't get things confused in your head 'bout what you might owe me later or how you're goin' to pay."

"Okay, Ridge. No promises then."

"No promises," he agreed. "But while I'm explainin' things, let me explain one more.

That was a mighty fine kiss an' I wouldn't mind havin' another, but only if you want to, an' only 'cause we're a man an' a woman together an' we like each other. Okay?"

Rosalie's smile brightened and her arms linked lightly around his neck as he lowered his lips to hers.

Chapter Four

It was almost midnight and Ridge decided it was time to start making a fool of himself. He was in the saloon Henry Lott had picked for him, Kelso's, which was a rowdy little whiskey den in the heart of the red light district of Adobe City.

The place was filled with a variety of hard-working, hard-drinking men, including miners just off from their shifts in the local mines, thirsty prospectors in from the mountains, rail splitters, railroad gang workers, freight handlers, and the like. Men were crowded shoulder-to-shoulder in the place, laughing, talking, and occasionally fighting, and the air inside was thick with noise and the stench of whiskey, cheap food, stale smoke, and vomit.

Ridge turned with his back to the bar and looked out over the room, not particularly looking forward to the fight he soon had to start. He had stayed with Rosalie Holley at their house until nearly ten o'clock, drinking coffee, talking, and thoroughly enjoying her company, but finally he knew he had to leave. They had parted with a final kiss, and then he had returned to his hotel room.

There he had reluctantly changed back into his filthy trail clothes, knowing he would fit in better in this part of town and in jail if he looked and smelled like just another rowdy, dirty roughneck. Then he packed all his belongings in the saddlebags and went down to the front desk to pay his bill and leave instructions about who would pick up his gear later. It would be awhile, he knew, before he was able to return to that comfortable hotel room.

Then he walked across town to the saloon district He had stopped in for drinks in a couple of other places before finally ending up at Kelso's where arrangements had been made for his arrest.

And now the time had come. He hitched up his trousers and started across the room toward the man he had chosen to take on. He was a big, burly fellow, easily topping 225 pounds, and Ridge picked him because he acted like somebody who had been in need of a good head cracking for some time. Earlier Ridge had seen him pick a fight with one of the miners who wandered in the saloon. After turning the miner's face to a bloody pulp with repeated blows from his massive fists, he had crushed the man's hand with a heavy boot heel and finally threw him bodily out the front doors into the street.

But as Ridge had watched the fight, he realized that all the big man had going for him was brute strength. He was drunk and ponderously slow. The miner he fought had been too near alcoholic oblivion himself to put up a good defense, but Ridge knew that a sober man who was quick enough to dodge those big meaty fists could easily defeat the big man.

Ridge pushed his way through the crowd and when he reached his chosen victim he drew his fist back and landed the first hard, unexpected blow. It jarred the big man back a couple of steps, but he did not go down. For a moment he just stood there, shaking his head to clear it as a low growl built up inside him. Then he grinned drunkenly at Ridge and launched himself clumsily forward, pawing bystanders out of the way like parting weeds.

Ridge waited on the charge, poising back on his right foot, and then at the last moment, he threw his full weight behind his swinging right fist. It connected with the big man's midsection and doubled him up, but his body still collided with Ridge and they both went down together. The breath almost left Ridge as the weight of his victim came down on top of him, but he hurriedly squirmed sideways and got in the clear.

Ridge rose to his feet and waited, his breath coming in pants now from the exertion, and his right hand throbbing from the blows he had delivered. The big man got to his hands and knees and looked around. When he spotted Ridge he started crawling forward, but Ridge laid him out again with a knee to the side of the head.

Then the stick struck. It was a glancing blow off the back of Ridge's head, and though it still hurt like hell, he could tell that whoever was behind him had held back on the blow at the last instant. He still fell, though, partly for effect and partly because he did not want to receive another rap on the skull from that stick, worthy cause or no.

Two men in the natty blue uniforms of the city police hauled Ridge roughly to his feet. He acted stunned and unsteady, and while one of the policemen took his pistol from his holster, the other turned to make sure the big man did not get up and renew the fight. Finally both took hold of Ridge's arms and started shoving their way through the crowd toward the door. A chorus of catcalls, laughter, and shouted insults accompanied them out into the street.

Outside they roughly parted a way through the jam of people who filled the street as they jostled Ridge away from the scene of the arrest. But finally, after rounding a couple of corners and starting down a quieter street, their firm grips on his upper arms relaxed and they returned their short oak clubs to their belts.

"Hope I didn't rap you too hard," one of them told Ridge as he led the way down an alley toward the center of town. "I ain't had much practice at clubbin' nobody I don't intend to hurt."

"It was plenty hard," Ridge said, rubbing the knot which had already risen on the back of his skull. "But I reckon it was somethin' you had to do."

"Yeah, it was, Marshal," the second policeman said, "an' I'm afraid there's more besides."

"More?" Ridge asked with a trace of dread in his voice.

"The cap'n told us to mark you up some," the man said with regret. "You know, like you got smart an' we had to rough you up 'fore we brought you in. He's afraid if you don't look beat up, them jailbirds might get suspicious."

"My friend Henry always thinks of everything," Ridge mumbled. He paused in the darkest part of the alley and turned to his two captors. "Wal, you might as well get it over with here an' now. But take care with the nose, okay? I kinda like it straight."

The two policemen looked at one another and then one of them stepped up to Ridge and said, "Guess I'm elected to do it. You ready?"

"As I'll ever be."

The policeman began to pop his face with a series of short hard jabs. They smarted, but they lacked the bone-jarring impact of real fighting punches, and the man concentrated his blows on Ridge's cheeks and chin, carefully avoiding his eyes and nose. He quit when he had drawn blood from a cut high up on Ridge's left cheek.

"That oughta do it," the policeman said at last, rubbing his chafed fists. "You're gonna look like hell in a couple of hours."

"Good," Ridge mumbled as he worked his jaw to loosen it up. "Then I'll look the way I feel already."

They walked on across town, and when they neared the courthouse, the two policemen again took hold of his arms to show he was in their custody. He struggled noisily with them as they started down the steep flight of outside steps toward the jail office, but they wrestled him down the stairs and through the heavy metal door.

The booking room was a fairly large one. In the center of the wall opposite the entrance was another metal door with a small barred window in it. On another wall was a long rack of rifles with a chain running through the trigger guards of each weapon. The only furniture in the place was a long scarred bench for waiting prisoners, three big desks and chairs, and a large metal cabinet where one of the policemen took Ridge's pistol and gunbelt to be locked up.

There were two jailers on duty, both big, sour-looking men, and when Ridge was brought in, one of them came over and opened the docket book to log him in.

"Drinkin' an' fightin' " one of the policemen told the jailer, who made a note in the book. "The usual."

The jailer looked up at Ridge an' said, "What's your name, tough guy?"

"Smith," Ridge mumbled, still playing the role of the rebellious drunk. He had no idea which of these men might know what was really going on and which did not.

The jailer got a tired expression on his

face and asked, "Got any papers with your name in them, Smith?"

"Nope. I ain't got nothin'."

"Well, whatever your name really is, we've got your ass an' you'll stay in the can 'til you can face the judge on Thursday mornin' an' pay your fine."

As the jailer was making his final entries into the docket, one of the policemen stepped up close behind Ridge and whispered to him, "That's the one you'll take out, over there in the red shirt. In about three hours. He'll go through once checking the doors an' the prisoners, an' when he comes back by, he'll pass close by your cell door."

Ridge didn't answer, but took a quick glance at the second jailer, who was lounged back in a chair across the room with a newspaper folded across his chest. Those were the same instructions Henry Lott had given him at Rosalie Holley's house.

In a moment the jailer took custody of Ridge and the two policemen left. He was led through the main lock-up door and down the long main aisle. The jail contained half a dozen cells on each side, most of which were full. Finally the jailer stopped in front of one cell and unlocked the door. The cell was about 10 feet square with stone walls on the back and both sides. It already contained four sleeping men.

The jailer shoved Ridge into the middle of the cell and slammed the door closed. Ridge whirled clumsily and came back to the bars, shouting oaths and threats at the top of his lungs. He succeeded in waking most of the men in the cell, who were sitting and lying in various places around the walls trying to rest.

But Ridge quieted when the jailer came back and said, "Either you shut your damn mouth an' go to sleep, or I'll come back here an' put you to sleep. You pick it, tough guy." He turned and marched away toward the front, and Ridge kept his mouth shut.

The only illumination in the cell area was one small lamp which hung from the ceiling about midway down the aisle between the long rows of cells. Ridge turned to survey the other prisoners, but he could make out little more than the dark forms of reclining men in the dim light. As they resettled themselves into their various sleeping positions, Ridge looked them over man by man, wondering how he would find out which were Blackie Crystal and Mexican Joe Rodriguez.

Then he noticed that one man was watching him intently, the whites of his small eyes seeming almost to glow through the darkness. He was sitting midway along one wall of the cell, and beside him was the prone figure of a second man.

Ridge turned toward the faint light and took the makings out of his shirt pocket. As he fumbled to roll a cigarette, he occasionally mumbled drunkenly to himself, cursing the police, the jailers, Adobe City, and everything else he could think of.

When he finished building the crumpled smoke, he searched his pockets uselessly for a match, then turned and looked around the cell. Spotting the man along the wall still watching him, he staggered over to him and said, "Gimme a match."

"Go to hell, *gringo,*" the man mumbled disinterestedly.

Now that he was closer, Ridge could tell more about the man he was talking to. He was only of medium size, but he had unusually broad shoulders and long, muscular arms like an ape's. The dark skin of his face was scarred and pitted, the apparent survivor of many fights and abuses, and he wore long mustaches which reached almost to the bottom of his chin. His eyes, shining in the lamplight as he gazed up at Ridge, were small and quick like a mink's, and his mouth was fixed in a permanent half snarl.

He was sitting with his knees pulled up to his chest and his arms folded across them. On one side of him lay a large black sombrero. It had to be Mexican Joe.

The man Ridge decided must be Blackie lay beside the Mexican, flat on his back with his arms folded over his chest and his long legs crossed. He wore an outfit which had probably once been dapper when it was clean and new, but the trousers and frilled white shirt were torn and filthy now, and the tooled leather vest was stained and ragged. He slept with his hat down across his eyes, and the Mexican seemed almost to be on guard beside him.

Ridge stared down at the Mexican a moment, weaving slightly, and then said, "Gimme a damn match, you lousy greaser."

Joe did not answer, but merely turned his head to the side and spat on the stone floor beside his hat. Ridge drew his foot back as if to land a kick, but the Mexican quickly grabbed his leg and twisted it. Ridge fell down hard, and in an instant Joe was on top of him and had both hands around his throat. "All right, then," Ridge managed to rasp out. "Don't gimme a match."

"You are lucky they take my knife, *bastardo*," Joe hissed through clenched teeth. "Maybe if I have it I cut off your nose and

61

feed it to you."

The other men in the cell, apparently drunks, were roused enough by the commotion to roll over and grumble about the noise, and the man lying beside the Mexican turned his head sideways, then raised up onto one elbow when he saw his companion sitting atop Ridge. "What's the trouble, Joe?" he asked.

"This *gringo,* he tries to be *mucho hombre,* and I show him he is not."

Ridge swung both fists up and crashed them into the side of Joe's head, and at the same time heaved his body upward and tumbled the Mexican sideways off of him. Then he jammed one knee hard up into Joe's stomach and, grabbing him by the hair, bashed his head against the wall a couple of times. Joe lay still.

When Ridge had taken the fight out of the Mexican, he quickly turned to Blackie, but Blackie seemed only amused by the fight. Ridge searched around on the floor and found his cigarette. It was broken in half, but he still stuck the best half in his mouth and asked Blackie, "You got a match?"

Blackie had a vague grin on his face. He produced a match from his vest pocket and gave it to Ridge, then picked up the second half of the cigarette and put it between his lips. Ridge lit his own smoke and then held the match out for Blackie.

"Ol' Joe's a pretty rough fighter," Blackie said as he took the first draw of smoke. "You're lucky you didn't run into him outside somewhere where he would have his knife on him."

"If he's so tough, how come he's out cold an' I'm here enjoyin' my smoke?" Ridge asked.

" 'Cause you're a sneaky fighter," Blackie said. "I like that."

"I win any way I can."

"Yeah, I can see that," Blackie grinned. "What you in this hole for?"

"Jus' bein' drunk," Ridge said. "I kicked a fat man's ass down by the tracks."

Blackie nodded, scarcely interested, and Ridge waited a moment before going on. This would be the hardest part, the time when he was most likely to arouse suspicion. "They don't know anything else 'bout me," he said, "an' I want to keep it that way."

"On the run, huh?"

Ridge turned and eyed Blackie with the dark suspicion of a drunk who suddenly senses threat. "Maybe," he said. "What you in here for?"

"Me an' Joe an' some of the boys robbed

a bank here in town," Blackie said without hesitation. "They jus' caught the two of us a few days ago. But I ain't sweatin' it. My men'll figure some way to get us out. Hell, it oughta be a cinch with only two jailers on duty out there at night. How 'bout you? What'd you do?"

"I needed me some money over in Three Pines," Ridge said, impulsively adopting the crime of Bill Deston. It would be a story that could be verified if necessary. "I took the express station there, but some damn law man got on my trail. I only lost him a couple of days ago up in the mountains. I stopped off here in town to blow it out, an' then I was headed down to see if I couldn't find that place they call The Havens." He looked around the cell suspiciously, and then said in a lower voice, "I'm still goin' soon's I can bust outa here."

Blackie chuckled quietly to himself and said, "You're bustin' out, huh? All by your lonesome?"

"It's the way I see it."

"This jail is tight," Blackie said. "It'll take friends on the outside. You got any?"

"Nope."

"Wal, maybe I'll take you with me when I go. We'll see. Maybe I won't, too. Ol'

64

Mexican Joe sure won't want you taggin' along."

"I ain't got to tag along with nobody," Ridge said angrily.

"Suit yourself," Blackie said, stubbing out the short butt he held and lying back down on the floor. Ridge got up and found himself a spot near the door of the cell. He sat down facing the big metal door to the jailer's room and leaned sideways against the bars.

He dozed off and on for the next couple of hours, never getting too comfortable or letting himself fall too deeply into sleep. Once he roused as Mexican Joe finally came to and moved back over beside Blackie. As the two of them talked in muted tones, the Mexican kept his eyes focused on Ridge in a venomous glare, but evidently Blackie ordered him not to come over and start any more trouble.

Joe was a man who would have to be dealt with when they got out of here, Ridge knew. The Mexican was not likely to forget how Ridge had whipped him, and Ridge figured him for a man who would take his revenge suddenly and savagely.

But still Ridge felt the fight was necessary. If he had come in here and started trying to make friends with Blackie and Joe, they would have been immediately suspicious of him. They were brutal men who understood only force and violence, and so he had chosen to deal with them on their own level. In whipping Joe, he had gained a grudging degree of respect from Blackie, and he believed that now they would trust him enough to go along when he made his break.

Ridge had drifted into a fairly deep sleep when he was awakened by the sound of the heavy iron door at the end of the aisle scraping open. He opened his eyes, but he did not move as the jailer came into view and started down the aisle, checking every door and looking in each cell at the sleeping men.

When he passed and had his back to Ridge, Ridge shifted around until his feet were under him, but he remained in a crouch. The jailer reached the end of the aisle and started back, still apparently unaware that any of the prisoners was awake and watching him. When he reached the door to the cell Ridge and the two outlaws were in, he grabbed one bar and shook the door to make sure it was locked tightly. As he did that, somehow the ring of keys he carried fell to the floor behind him.

The jailer turned and bent to retrieve the keys, and as he was straightening up, Ridge went into action. One of his arms snaked out through the bars and looped about the jailer's throat, pulling him back suddenly against the bars, while the other hand clamped tightly over his mouth. The jailer thrashed around clumsily, his fingers digging at Ridge's arm in a useless attempt to escape the strangle hold, but Ridge kept his arm tight, knowing he could black the man out in a moment without doing him any permanent harm.

Almost instantly, Mexican Joe Rodriguez was at Ridge's side, reaching through the bars for the jailer's keys, and a second later Blackie came over, too, and grabbed the pistol from the jailer's holster.

It all happened so quickly and quietly that neither of the other prisoners in the cell were even roused from their sleep. As the jailer finally went limp, Ridge let him slump to the stone floor and Joe quickly reached out and stuck a key in the lock. It took a minute to open the door as the Mexican frantically tried several keys before finally finding the right one.

As the door to freedom swung open in front of them, Ridge turned to Blackie and whispered cynically, "You gonna let me tag along on your big escape, mister?"

Without answering, Blackie stepped through the doorway and motioned with the gun for the others to follow him. That gun worried Ridge. He had hoped to get his own hands on it first because he knew that Blackie was likely to kill somebody on the way out.

Before they reached the big door to the jailer's outer office, Ridge caught Blackie's arm and stopped him for a moment. "No shootin' 'less you have to," he cautioned the outlaw. "One shot is likely to bring more law men out of the woodwork than we know what to do with."

Blackie nodded his agreement and went on. He sprang through the door and caught the second jailer completely off guard, and Ridge and Joe were close behind him.

Ridge disarmed the second jailer and pointed the man's own pistol at him. "Where's the guns?" he demanded.

The jailer, who had probably been ordered not to oppose them in any way, turned and unlocked the large metal cabinet.

Ridge found his own pistol and gunbelt inside there and quickly strapped them on. He also took the best of the Winchesters he found, and then turned to hold a gun on the jailer as Blackie and Mexican Joe armed themselves. When they were finished, Ridge said, "Put all the extra guns inside there an' lock it back. We'll take the keys with us." While their backs were turned, Ridge popped the jailer in the head with the butt of the Winchester. The blow was not hard enough to crack the shell of a decent walnut, but the jailer still dropped like a dead man and lay still on the floor.

"Check the door, Joe," Blackie ordered as he examined the load in his revolver. The Mexican moved to the door, gun drawn, and peeked outside, then turned and motioned for the others to come on.

The moon had long since gone down and it was pitch black in the alley beside the courthouse. The three of them went cautiously toward the front of the building with Joe in the lead. At this early morning hour, the street was deserted, but a short distance away, two saddled horses were tied to the rail front of a shop. Across the street and a little farther away was a third horse.

Mexican Joe and Blackie dashed over to the two horses, and Ridge hurried down the street to the third. When he neared it, he noticed with a flash of appreciation to Henry Lott that it was his own mount, President Grant.

They all three mounted and raced south out of town. But once they had left the occasional street lamps of Adobe City behind, the riding became treacherous and they were forced to slow the horses to a walk.

"I figger," Ridge said as he drew up beside Blackie, "that we got as much as ten or fifteen minutes 'fore they discover the break. But it's so dark that they won't be able to start any serious trackin' 'til dawn, maybe two hours from now."

"We'll be long gone by then," Blackie chuckled. "We're obliged to you for gettin' us outa there, mister. By the way, what's your name, anyway?"

"It's Rich Parks, but I mostly just go by Parks."

"Okay, thanks, Parks. Where would you be headin' now?"

"I still had me a mind to head down to them Havens if I can find 'em," Ridge said.

"Then ride with us," Blackie offered. "We're goin' there, an' maybe on the way we can talk a little more 'bout this gang I got. I'm always on the lookout for smart hombres with a strong streak of bastard in 'em."

"An' who might you be?"

"The handle's Blackie Crystal, an' that there's Mexican Joe Rodriguez, my *segundo*." The Mexican did not turn to acknowledge the introduction.

"I've heard of you," Ridge allowed. "But I thought you was down Texas way."

"We was," Blackie admitted vaguely, "an'

70

now we're up Colorado way. You comin'?"

"Reckon so."

CHAPTER FIVE

They rode hard all the next day. Mexican Joe kept the lead and set the pace, pushing the stolen horse he rode without mercy. Ridge hated to work his own President Grant so hard this soon after the grueling crossing over the mountains, but he knew it was necessary for him to keep up with the two outlaws, and he was confident that his big strong mount was equal to the task. When they reached The Havens, the horse could rest for several days with very little riding.

Because they had no food, their few brief stops during the day were only to drink at the occasional streams and lakes they passed, and to let the horses blow and grab a few bites of grass.

Ridge had hoped they would stop sometime after sunset, but the two outlaws had no way of knowing that a posse would not be close behind them, and so they kept riding on into the night by the light of the clear bright moon which soon rose in the sky.

At last, though, they were forced to stop for a while. They had been following a treacherous, winding trail up a mountain-side for about an hour, riding single file along the ragged pathway with Joe still in the lead and Ridge bringing up the rear. In one place the four-foot-wide trail rose sharply upward with a solid wall of ragged rock on one side and a drop of more than 200 feet on the other. Suddenly Mexican Joe's horse, the weakest and tiredest of the three mounts, hit a patch of loose gravel and shale, and its hooves slid out from under it. With a startled squeal, the animal fell sideways, and horse and rider went down, sliding awkwardly back down the trail for several feet.

At last the Mexican was able to scramble clear and get his footing, and then he began to tug on the reins of his fallen mount until it too had stopped sliding. As the frantic animal began to scramble desperately to its feet, the infuriated Joe began to pound its nose with his fist and curse it with vile Spanish condemnations. His fury was such that he scarcely seemed to notice that both he and the mount were still dangerously close to toppling off the edge of the trail and falling to their deaths.

Finally Blackie, who had ridden up close and was having difficulty calming his own horse, snapped out, "Dammit, Joe! Cut it out!"

The Mexican quit beating the animal then, but his stream of oaths continued as he attempted to maneuver it around to a position where he could remount.

Ridge had paused farther down the trail, watching the whole scene with calm disdain. Finally he said, "Either you stop for a while or you'll be on foot within an hour. Ain't no use beatin' a horse that jus' fell down 'cause you've rode it 'til it's half dead."

Joe paused and shot a quick hateful glance back in Ridge's direction. He was still having trouble mounting because each time he tried to step around to the horse's side, it edged away from him. And each step kept both horse and rider constantly close to the dangerous precipice. The horse was bleeding along one front shoulder and was favoring one leg, but nothing seemed to be broken.

"If I lose this horse," the Mexican hissed at Ridge, "maybe I just get myself another one *pronto*."

"Yeah," Ridge drawled, "an' maybe you stay out here in the mountains as dead as

74

the horse you killed."

"That's enough," Blackie interrupted. "You two are goin' to have plenty of time to bristle up an' talk tough once we get back to The Havens. I don't want to hear no more of it 'til we put some more distance between us and them nooses they got waitin' for us back there. You got that?"

Neither of the other two men answered him, but Joe turned and began leading his fatigued horse on up the trail. When they reached a place where the trail widened out and leveled off for a short distance, he was finally able to remount.

Within fifteen minutes, Blackie had chosen a spot for them to stop for a while. It was an area where the rocks and boulders clustered around a small clearing about 15 feet across, and though there was no water or grass for the horses, it was the best they could do at the time.

Ridge volunteered to take the watch. He would not have been able to sleep much anyway, knowing that Mexican Joe was nearby and would like nothing better than to kill him as he slept. They unsaddled their horses and tied them nearby, and then as the two outlaws were spreading bedrolls on the ground, Ridge took his rifle and climbed up on one of the boulders overlooking the way they had just come.

He chose that spot as much because it was in sight of where Joe and Blackie lay as for any other reason. He knew that guarding against the attack of a posse was unnecessary since Lott would not be following along after them this soon. The captain knew where The Havens were and he knew that was where the escaped prisoners would head to. But he would not put much heat on them until Ridge had some time to locate Billy Dean Holley and try to save him.

Ridge sat down with his back against a rock, his knees pulled up to his chest for warmth, and his rifle cradled in his lap. He stayed that way for several hours, shifting only occasionally to stretch his limbs and work the stiffness out of his back. But close to dawn, he finally drifted off to sleep, his head lolling slowly backward until it rested on the rock behind him.

When he woke, he knew he had not been asleep long, but he sensed that something was already different, somehow wrong. Without moving, he opened his eyes and looked cautiously around him. The first grayness of dawn was just beginning to define the shapes of things around him, and he noticed with a sudden rush of tension that only one man now lay against the rocks across the small clearing below him.

Slowly and silently, Ridge raised his head, straightened his legs and eased the rifle up into both hands, ready to be snapped up and fired instantly.

A long quiet moment passed, and then he heard the crunch of a footstep behind some rocks close by and to the right of him. He turned the muzzle of the rifle in that direction and waited.

There was no more noise in that direction, but he was sure it was Mexican Joe back in the shadows between two of the large rocks. "Step out careful, like, an' let me take a look at you," he said.

His words roused Blackie, who immediately sat up and reached for his pistol. "It's me," Joe said from the recesses. "You let me take a damn pee and don't shoot. Okay?"

Ridge did not answer, though he doubted that nature's urgings was the reason that the Mexican had left his bedroll and moved over so silently in this direction. In a moment Joe stepped out from the shadows, buttoning his pants, and went back over to his bedroll.

"Since we're awake anyway," Blackie said, turning back his blankets and rising, "we might as well head out."

Since they had no breakfast to prepare or coffee to boil, it took them only minutes to saddle up and leave, but by the time they started on up the trail, the approaching morning had already grown bright enough for them to see the way ahead clearly. Mexican Joe set an easier pace this morning, both because of the condition of his horse and because from these heights, they could see far down their back trail. Nobody was following them.

They rode due west for nearly two hours, topping the mountain and working their way down the opposite side. Then Joe turned his horse south, following the contours of a long narrow valley.

By midmorning they had arrived at a clear blue mountain lake, and they stopped again there for about half an hour to let the horses water and eat some of the thick green grass which grew in patches around the lake. Then they continued on down the valley.

Before noon Ridge caught his first glimpse of the sun's rays reflecting off some shiny object far in the distance and he knew they must be close to The Havens. That glimmer of reflection, he guessed, was one of the first sentries watching them through field glasses.

In about twenty minutes they neared the position of the sentry, but he never made his presence known and neither of the two outlaws cast a glance up in the direction of the high cliff where he was stationed. But below the sentry's high vantage point, the trail again turned west and began climbing up through a narrow pass which led up a mountainside. Ridge could see that there had been a fair bit of horse traffic through here recently, and that the pass seemed to be well worn. There were even some ruts which indicated the occasional passage of wagons through here, though it amazed Ridge to think that anybody could manage to navigate a wagon through these mountains.

He spotted another guard far off in the distance, but that man, too, was out of sight by the time they neared him. All the guards, Ridge figured, must know Blackie and Mexican Joe on sight.

Joe led them through a jumbled mass of house-sized boulders, and when they reached the other side, suddenly they were in The Havens.

The long valley was oval-shaped, perhaps half a mile long and over a quarter of a mile wide. The walls on all sides rose steeply upward, prohibiting any entrance or exit from the place except past the guards who were posted along the cliffs above the pass.

About a dozen buildings were clustered in a row along one side with their hacks to a sheer wall of stone which rose straight up for a couple of hundred feet. They presented the general appearance of a crude little mountain settlement, that could just as easily have been a mining camp or a trading outpost as an outlaw stronghold. There was one large, fortified log building two stories high, with battlements on the roof similar to the guard tower of a fort, and the remainder of the buildings were squat log cabins stretched out in two rows on either side of it.

The buildings were bunched up on the high side of the valley, and beyond them were two large corrals which held a few horses. As many as twenty more horses and a few head of cattle were grazing peacefully in the center of the valley.

As they rode up toward the large main building, men began to appear from inside it, as well as from a few of the cabins, to greet Blackie and Mexican Joe. When they stopped their horses in front of the large building and stepped to the ground, a short, graying bear of a man came out the front door and over to the edge of the porch to shake Blackie's hand.

"It's damned good to see you two back,

Blackie," the man said in a deep bass voice which seemed to roll out of his chest like thunder. "The note must of worked an' they let you out." A smile showed through his bushy mat of whiskers.

"I don't know nothin' about no note," Blackie said. "We busted out."

"Nice goin' Blackie," the man said. "We didn't think they'd pay that note no mind nohow, but we went ahead an' tried it anyway."

"What note you talkin' about, Char?" Blackie finally asked.

"Well, see, we made up this letter an' said we'd kill that marshal feller we got 'less they let you an' the Mex out of jail," the man called Char said. "I sent one of your men in town with it three days ago an' he mailed it to that head marshal there."

"You got a marshal here?" Blackie asked happily. "How'd you get your hands on 'im?"

"Hell, we had us two of them, Blackie," one of the other men said proudly. "They was in the posse that chased us after the bank job. But we didn't want to bother with no two prisoners so we jus' hung one of 'em up to dry. The other one's tied up back in Char's tack shed."

Ridge looked at this man closely, wanting

to remember who he was for later. He was a tall, thin man with dull features and thick, unruly black hair.

"Good goin', Carter," Blackie grinned. "Later on we'll have us some fun with 'im, soon's ol' Joe here can steal himself another hog sticker."

"I get one soon," Joe vowed with a crooked grin.

"Who's this you brought with you?" Char asked, taking a close look at Ridge for the first time.

"Name's Parks," Blackie said. "Parks, this here's Char Binnaker, the sort of landlord of these Havens. He'll charge you goin' an' comin' every time you take a leak around this place, but he ain't such a bad ol' sonofabitch once you get to know him."

Binnaker took Ridge's hand with a grip that could crush rocks and said, "Good meetin' you, Parks." But after the greeting, he was suddenly all business as he began to lay down the rules of his domain. "A cot in a cabin is worth two dollars a night, ten a week. Meals is a dollar apiece. Whiskey an' beer's a dollar, an' women is six dollars a night. If you sleep out an' eat your own grub, it's a dollar a day for breathin' my air. You got guard duty from midnight to eight, an' if you break my rules or try to run out on a debt here, I'll tie your tail to that pole over there an' skin you out like a catfish. Got any questions?"

"That seems to plumb cover it," Ridge grinned. "The way I see it, I can afford to stay 'round here maybe all afternoon 'fore my poke runs out."

"Naw, it's all right, Parks," Blackie assured him. Then, turning to Binnaker, he added, "Parks is joinin' up with my outfit, so you don't worry 'bout him, Char. He helped me an' Joe break out an' he's all right."

"If you say so, Blackie," Binnaker agreed. "Hell, that might even call for one free at the bar an' one in the sack. Come on into the big house an' I'll start pourin'."

Blackie instructed one of the men there to take care of their horses, and Ridge followed along as everyone else moved inside the big log building. The main room on the ground floor of the building was a combination saloon, café, and general store, an arrangement which was common in small settlements and trading posts all over. Along the back wall was the long bar with its kegs of beer and whiskey and stock of glasses and mugs. At one end of the room was a counter and several shelves covered with basic necessities such as canned food, ammunition, and blankets, and at the other end was a stairway leading to the second floor. The center of the main room was filled with tables and chairs, and behind one end of the bar was a doorway which led to a kitchen and living quarters in back.

Blackie took a chair at the largest table in the place like a monarch preparing to hold court, and the rest of the ten to twenty men there gathered around him. Binnaker went around behind the bar to begin pouring drinks, and in a moment a young Indian woman quietly appeared from the back room to help him.

"That's Char's squaw," Blackie explained to Ridge, who had taken a seat beside him. "An' if you know what's good for you, you leave her be, Ridge. After we got here 'bout a month ago, I seen him take some young kid out to the pole an' skin him alive 'cause the boy decided he wanted to try out some of that squaw stuff. It wasn't wise of him a'tall, 'cause 'ol Char, he ain't a very understandin' man."

"What's mine is mine," Binnaker called out from over at the bar.

"Yeah," one of the other men laughed, "an' what some other feller's got is yours, too, whenever you think you can take it." Everybody got a good laugh out of that.

"I'll keep it in mind," Ridge said with a grin.

"You do that," Blackie said. "If you get to feelin' the need, there's another squaw an' some Mex women 'round here. They're pigs, mostly, but they're better'n a poke in the eye with a sharp stick."

"They're good enough for your kind," Char said as he set a bottle and glasses on the table, and the rest of the men laughed along with him.

Ridge accepted the drink he was given and joined in the celebration of Blackie's return for a while, though his body was telling him that it had been much too long since he had last eaten and slept. Binnaker's whiskey was acrid and bitter and it hit his empty stomach like a steel ball in a balloon.

He could see immediately that this was a rough crowd he had thrown in with, a lowly collection of saddle tramps and killers, crude hard men whose only values had to do with money, liquor, women, and the comradeship of the gang. Ridge could quickly tell that Blackie Crystal was the strong forceful influence necessary to keep such a lot under control and ready to do his bidding. He dominated the group, laughing and carrying on, and yet still expecting his most offhanded orders to be carried out immediately and without question.

Ridge paid close attention when the talk turned to the capture of Mark Franklin and Billy Dean Holley. As four men began to tell their boss how they had hung Franklin, Ridge memorized who they were and began to focus his attention mainly on them. In addition to his job of freeing Holley and taking Blackie back, he vowed to himself that these four men would not get away. One by one he picked their names out in the conversation. Stone. Lattershaw. Teller. Carter.

His concentration was interrupted when the Indian woman came to him and said, "Mister. Char say bring food you."

Ridge watched as a plate of roast meat and beans was set on the table in front of him. "I been needin' this bad," he said, smiling his appreciation up at the woman. Then as she set similar meals in front of Blackie and Mexican Joe, Ridge looked her over more closely, this woman that Char Binnaker skinned people over.

She was a short, heavy-breasted woman with strong-looking arms and shoulders, and dark, reddish brown skin. She was obviously young, not more than twenty-five, but hard living had etched a permanent look of sadness and dull resignation on a face that might otherwise have been vaguely pretty. She wore an ancient grease-splotched buckskin dress that might once have been attractive long ago, and her waist-length black hair was pulled straight back on her head and tied with a short piece of cord.

Ridge accepted the bent fork she offered and went to work immediately on the food.

When the meal was finished, Ridge left the table and went back to the bar where Binnaker was. "I ain't closed my eyes for more'n an hour in the last two days," he said, "an' I think I'm gonna die standin' up if I don't get some sleep."

"Sure, Parks. The third cabin down the east row ain't got nobody in it right now. You take that one. An' grab yourself a blanket on your way out if you ain't got one. I'll charge Blackie for it, or you can pay me later."

Ridge got a blanket and left the building. As he plodded down toward the vacant cabin, he felt a pang of guilt because he was heading off to sleep while somewhere nearby, probably within shouting distance, was a fellow marshal who had probably been tied up for days and might soon face the carving skills of Mexican Joe if Ridge did not do something about it first.

But just then rest was a necessity for

Ridge. He had driven his body too hard for too long, and he could not take the risk of having his mind or his strength fail him sometime over the next critical few days.

When he reached the cabin, the plank door was slightly ajar, and Ridge had to put his shoulder against it to shove it open wide enough to get in. The two windows inside were covered with heavy wooden shutters, and he opened one slightly to let some light and fresh air in, then returned and forced the door closed.

The ten-by-ten cabin was the crudest of structures. The walls were of unchinked logs and the floor was dirt. In back was a small fireplace of stone and mud mortar, and on each of the side walls were two bunks built of planks with straw ticks.

Ridge spread the blanket on the lower bunk opposite the open window, removed his shirt, and sat down. He pulled off his boots, then took off his gunbelt and laid it at the head of the bunk so the butt of his pistol would be right by his face while he was sleeping.

Finally he went over and closed the shutters of the window and returned to flop down onto the bed. He was asleep almost instantly.

■ ■ ■ ■

The voice was low but insistent. It invaded Ridge's sleep like an unwanted intruder. He rolled over onto his back, returning slowly to wakefulness, and instinctively his hand sought the handle of the revolver.

"*Señor*," the female voice called from outside. "*Señor?*"

"What is it?" Ridge growled, irritated at being awakened.

"It is Maria, *señor.* I come in. Okay?"

"Yeah, yeah. Come on in."

The door scraped slowly open, letting in a flood of unwanted sunlight, and a young woman stepped inside and looked around.

"The *patrón,*" she said, spotting Ridge on the cot and coming over to him. "He tell me come here and make pleasure for you."

Then, with complete casualness, she began to unbutton the front of her filthy cotton dress. She was a drab Mexican woman of about thirty with a fleshy, homely face and the chubby body of someone who has lived their life on a diet of cheap, starchy food. Her black hair hung in greasy ropes across her shoulders and down her back, and she carried with her a strong body odor, separate and distinct, but equally as strong as Ridge's own.

Caught off guard, he watched for a moment as she opened the front of her dress, but he caught her hand and stopped her before she could reach up and slip the filthy shapeless garment clear of her shoulders. "Wait! Don't do that!" he said quickly.

She stopped then and looked down at Ridge in confusion. "The *patrón, Señor* Binnaker, he say no pay one time. You help Blackie. No pay for Maria one time."

Ridge considered the dilemma for a moment. The thought of being with a woman who was available to all the other scum in this place disgusted him, and yet he knew he could not get rid of her by simply sending her away. That would be out of character with the role he was playing. This woman's presence here was part of his rites of entry into this crude, animalistic society he had been thrust into, and when she returned and began telling how he had not wanted her, it would undoubtedly put him under a cloud of suspicion. These men seldom turned down any woman, no matter what size, shape, age, or degree of willingness.

"Un momento" he said, leaving the half-dressed woman standing there by the bed as he rose and crossed the room to open the window. It gave him an instant to think,

and when he turned and came back to her, he was fishing in his pants pocket. He pulled out a five-dollar gold piece and handed it to Maria.

"I've got me a secret, Maria," he said as he reached out and pulled the front of her dress back together, indicating that he wanted her to button it back up. "You savvy secret?"

She nodded her understanding as she eagerly examined the piece of money and made it quickly disappear somewhere inside her clothing.

"I was hurt in the war," Ridge went on, trying to sound sad and ashamed. "I can't . . . nothin' happens when I'm with a woman. Even with a pretty one like you."

Maria's expression became sympathetic as she suddenly understood what he was saying. "You no make happy . . . ever?"

"I can't," Ridge told her quietly. "But I don't want the others to know. They'd only poke fun at me an' pretty soon I'd get around to killin' somebody over it. Will you help me keep my secret, Maria?"

"*Si.* I keep," Maria promised, patting the stashed piece of gold. She turned as if to leave, but Ridge reached out and took hold of her arm.

"Wait," he said. "If you go back now,

they'll know nothin' happened. You stay an' talk to me for a while, an' then go back. Okay?"

"I stay," Maria smiled. As Ridge sat down on the edge of the bed, she dropped down and sat on the ground at his feet, rubbing his leg gently. "Poor cowboy," she said quietly, and she seemed almost on the verge of tears in sympathy for him.

But Ridge wanted to get off that subject as quickly as possible. He decided that as long as he had her here, he might as well try and get a little information from her.

"How long have you lived here, Maria?" he asked.

She thought for a moment, apparently grasping for an understanding of his question, and finally she said, "Me live here? *Uno, dos* . . . two . . ." She held up two fingers and searched for a word.

"Two years?"

"*Si.* Two years. When I come here, the *patrón,* he kill my man and take me. Then I *patrón*'s woman. Then she come. Now he have Indian bitch and Maria is every man's woman."

"How many men are here right now?" Ridge asked. "How many men stay here?"

Maria thought for a moment and then held up all ten fingers to Ridge. "This many," she said. She closed her fists and then held up all her fingers again. "And maybe this many."

Twenty men, Ridge thought. A good defensive force for a secure little valley like this.

"And how many women?"

"Three, and Maria and the Indian bitch." Ridge was beginning to get the strong impression that Maria did not think very much of the young squaw who was Char Binnaker's current woman, and he thought she probably hated Char just as much for casting her aside for the use of his many customers. He decided to store that conclusion away for possible future use.

"Twenty men and five women," Ridge said, "and one prisoner. One law man."

"*Si.* Poor Holley. Maybe he die soon, die bad from Mexican Joe." Ridge smiled to himself, pleased by the significance of Maria's knowing Billy Dean's name. She must have seen him and talked to him, and it was evident that she liked the young marshal enough to feel sorrow over his predicament.

"Where is Holley?" Ridge asked.

"In the little house for horses," she said. She held her wrists together behind her back and said, "Always like this. Poor Holley."

"Yeah, poor Holley."

After a reasonable length of time, Ridge let Maria leave and return to the main house, but not before making her repeat her promise not to tell the others about his "problem." As a final incentive, he told Maria he wanted her to come back and see him again and that he would give her more gold. With the sympathy she had seemed to show for the captive marshal, and with little else to go on, Ridge began to think that this Mexican *puta* might somehow become the key to arranging Holley's escape.

CHAPTER SIX

Ridge wanted to sleep for a while longer, but he had too much on his mind to go back to sleep. He could hardly believe he had actually infiltrated The Havens and was here now, surrounded by some of the most deadly outlaws in the central Rockies.

Places like The Havens cropped up occasionally, usually organized and managed by shrewd customers like Binnaker, hut generally their spans of existence were limited, thriving for two or three or four years until somebody somewhere had had enough and put together a force of law men and soldiers large enough to battle their way in and clean them out.

Before he came here, Ridge had known of The Havens, but only in general terms as a place where, if your quarry reached it, you might as well forget it and turn back. Several reckless law men had died trying to get in this place and get back out alive.

Char Binnaker was a reasonably ambiguous figure. Henry Lott had told Ridge he believed Binnaker was one of the raiders in William Quantrill's band during the war. Quantrill had assembled a gang of lawless guerilla fighters and had operated loosely under the guise of Confederate sympathizers to terrorize northwest Missouri and western Kansas during the early 1860s.

After the war it was believed that Binnaker had tried to form a gang of his own, but he could not make a go of it. He had disappeared for several years, but a couple of years before, it was learned that he was the moving force behind The Havens, and from what Ridge had already seen, he guessed that this had become a far more lucrative enterprise than holding up banks and robbing trains.

But the end of The Havens was near now. They had gone too far and brought on the wrath of the wrong people. Following the humiliating death of Mark Franklin, Ridge knew that not a single marshal in the state would be satisfied until this place was raided and Blackie Crystal's gang was wiped out.

Areas like the Colorado Rockies were still wide-open, lawless, and dangerous, but Ridge knew that the times were slowly changing, and the days when bands of men like the one Crystal led could rob and kill with impunity were coming to an end.

About dark Ridge rose and dressed. Although it felt safe and comfortable in the little cabin, he knew he was not here to enjoy either of those luxuries, and he had to get out and start doing the job he had come here to do.

He made his way back up to the large main building. Most of the crowd, including Blackie and Mexican Joe, were in their cabins, and there were only three men in the front room of the big house. Two were sitting at a table to one side, nursing their expensive drinks, and the third, Binnaker, was sitting behind the bar honing the blade of a large knife.

When Ridge reached the bar, Binnaker put the knife down and said, "What'll it be, Parks?"

Ridge dropped a dollar on the bar and said, "Beer." As Binnaker was drawing the mug of warm beer from a keg behind the bar, Ridge told him, "Thanks for the woman, Binnaker."

"Wal, Blackie's a good customer," Binnaker said. "He spends a lot of money here an' I was glad to get 'im back."

"I didn't know 'im when we was in jail," Ridge admitted. "He an' the Mexican just sorta came along when I busted out. But about that Maria. Don't she ever take a bath? She stinks like last year's outhouse."

"What the hell do you expect in a place like this?" Binnaker asked offhandedly. "Lily Langtry for six bucks?"

"S'pose not."

"Maria come here with a burnt out ol' drunk that used to be some kind of hotshot *bandito* down south. He had himself a high ol' time an' then tried to take off in the middle of the night still owin' me a couple of hundred." Binnaker held up the shiny blade of his knife and said, "Ain't nobody been able to do that yet. The girl, she's jus' a stupid peon, but she's earned me back all the money the ol' man owed . . . an' then some. Men ain't too choosey when they're on the run an' come to hide out here."

Ridge nodded his understanding and took a swallow of the beer. Binnaker watched him for a moment and then said, "Rich Parks. I don't recollect ever hearin' that name before. Where you work at mostly?"

"I been over in Kansas mostly for the last few years. Some down in Oklahoma an' Texas, but that job I pulled in Three Pines was the first I've done in Colorado for years. Maybe the last, too. Alls I got was $84. Can you believe that? An' I had to shoot two

98

men to get that."

"Work alone?"

"Mostly. I rode some with Mac Firston durin' the war, but the Yankees made it too hot on his bunch finally, an' I took off. Lucky thing, too. I heard later they come West here an' got in the middle of some damn range war somewhere. The whole crew was wiped out."

"Yeah. In Trinity Wells, over on the far side. I heard about it, too."

Again Ridge had borrowed from actual facts to fabricate an outlaw background for himself. He actually had ridden with Firston's gang, but as a government agent assigned to gather evidence on Firston and his Confederate Army boss, Major Lester Salem. Later, near Trinity Wells, he had arrested both men and provided the testimony that it took to put them in federal prison.

"Since the war I mostly jus' worked alone," Ridge said. "That way I know I'm keepin' company I can trust." Though the conversation seemed casual enough, Ridge knew there was a purpose behind it. He had expected this sort of interrogation from somebody, Binnaker, Blackie, or somebody, and he had prepared a believable background for himself in his mind.

"That mean you ain't joinin' Blackie like

he thinks?" Binnaker asked.

"No, I reckon I am," Ridge said. "The law's hot on me an' I need a stake. This eighty-four dollars won't get me nowhere. Prob'ly I won't even get out of this valley with none of it. But I figger with the big jobs Blackie pulls, my share should be enough to get me somewhere new where the law men ain't all heard of me. Maybe California or Nevada or someplace like that. I don't know."

"It gets pretty tough 'round here sometimes," Binnaker said. "We ain't never had none of 'em in here, but them damn marshals can dog a man like an' Injun. That's why it pleasures me that we got that one out there. Blackie says we'll have a party tomorrow night, an' maybe the next mornin' that marshal won't be 'round no more."

Ridge tried not to react to that piece of news, but it was a startling revelation. That meant he had only one night and a day to arrange Holley's escape.

He quickly changed the subject as if the topic of killing a marshal held no interest for him. " 'Bout that guard duty, Binnaker," he said. "What's that all about?"

"Every man that stays here pulls duty up on the rocks above the pass. We watch it all the time so can't no law men nor troops sneak in here an' catch us unawares."

"So what do I do?"

"Bill an' Slim over there," Binnaker said, pointing to the men at the table across the room. "They got the same shift as you do an' they'll show you the ropes. You jus' take your Winchester an' watch that pass. We always let one or two men in without bother-in' 'em 'cause if they're the law we can deal with 'em here, but anything over two, you pick up that rifle an' start blastin' like hell.

"One other thing, too. Nobody leaves at night 'less I told you before you went out that they were leavin'. Anybody starts out at night, you take 'em alive if you can an' bring 'em back to me. I take 'em to the pole."

Again Binnaker flourished the knife for emphasis. It seemed to Ridge that this big man enjoyed being the sole authority, the judge, jury, and lawmaker here, and he seemed to particularly relish also being the local executioner.

"No prisons an' no appeals, huh?" Ridge asked.

"Jus' the pole an' then the bone pile," Bin-naker said sternly.

Parkman talked to Binnaker awhile longer, then took his beer over and sat down with the two men at the table. Neither were members of Blackie Crystal's gang, but Ridge recognized the name of one of the men, Slim Bettermore, as that of a man wanted for a rape in Denver and an armed robbery in Boulder.

Neither of the men was friendly or talkative, so after making sure one of them would stop by his cabin and wake him for guard duty, he got up and went outside. He had said he was going back to the cabin to sleep awhile longer, but he actually wanted to use the darkness to do some scouting around. He still had not found out exactly where the captive marshal, Billy Holley, was being held, and he also wanted to take a closer look at some parts of the valley to see if there might be a second hidden entrance to it. There was not much time left, and he was going to have to set up a plan and put it in action quickly. Otherwise, it would be too late to save Holley.

He ducked around the side of the big log building and hurried through the shadows to the back. Behind the building was an outhouse, a large woodpile, a shed, and a pump. The shed was small and dilapidated and Ridge doubted that Holley was being kept there, but he still eased over to it and looked inside. It was filled with kegs and cases of empty liquor bottles.

Next Ridge started away toward the back of the nearest cabin. He remembered that one man had described the place Holley was as a "tack shed" and Maria had called it the "house for horses" so Ridge decided that it was probably somewhere down near the corrals. There was no real barn in the settlement, but he figured there was probably some sort of tack shed where the men could leave their saddles and other gear in out of the weather.

He worked his way quickly but cautiously down the rear of the line of cabins. Voices came out of a couple of them and in one he saw the glow of lamplight, but none of them had windows on the back and so he made it to the last one without detection.

From there he spotted the dark shape of a small building about 100 feet away near the first of the corrals. He considered the situation a moment and decided that it might be dangerously suspicious to be seen dashing out of the darkness toward the small building, so he just calmly walked across the open space to it.

When he neared the building, he began to hear the faint sound of voices inside and when he got close enough to peek through a crack in the boards he saw that someone was in there with Holley.

At first he could only make out the dark shape of a woman with her back to him, but when he heard her mutter "Poor Holley," he knew who it was. Ridge worked his way around to the far side of the structure and found another crack to look through.

Billy Holley was leaning against the back wall of the shed, trussed up like a wild bull waiting for slaughter. A rope had been tied around his ankles, then looped round and round his legs before finally coming up to secure his hands tightly behind his back. A gag had apparently been tied around his mouth, but Maria had it down now as she spoon fed him some concoction from a wooden bowl.

Holley looked like hell. His face was a mass of bruises and cuts from the abuse he had received from the outlaws, and his eyes in the dim lamplight had a sunken, crazed look, probably from spending so many miserably uncertain days tied up in the shed.

Between mouthfuls of food, he was talking to Maria in a low, urgent whisper. "Maria, you've gotta help me get away. Please."

"No, no," the woman insisted. "Poor Holley. They kill Maria if she help. Binnaker tie me on the pole."

"Just untie me before you go," Holley

pleaded. "I'm goin' crazy out here. Just loosen the ropes a little. Nobody will know you did it."

As the girl jammed another spoonful of food into his mouth to quiet him, she said insistently, "He know."

When Holley could speak again, he said, "When I get away, I'll come back with plenty of men and kill Binnaker. I'll get you out of this place."

That idea seemed to interest Maria more and she hesitated before answering. But she was still too frightened to offer him any encouragement. "If you gone, the *patrón,* he kill me right now." She made a motion down the front of her body like an imaginary knife making a long gash in her flesh. Then she shuddered and shoved more food at Holley.

Ridge watched for a moment longer, then moved away. He skirted the corrals and then started across the open area beyond. He was far enough away from the buildings now that he did not worry about being seen or heard, but he knew he must still hurry before somebody noticed his absence and began looking for him. He estimated that he had no more than two hours before Bill and Slim went to the cabin to get him for guard duty.

He moved as quickly as he could over the rough, rocky stretch to the back side of the valley about 200 yards from the corrals. There he began looking for any sizable openings in the rocks or anything which seemed like it might be a back trail out of the place. He searched without success for half an hour before finally coming across one place that looked interesting.

It was an opening in the rocks about the width of a man's shoulders. Ridge started into it cautiously, expecting it to reach a dead end at any moment, but it kept going on and on, rising sharply in some places and turning abruptly in others, but always passable to a man on foot. Ridge knew that not even a small, agile horse would be able to pass through some of the narrower parts of the path, which ruled out the possibility of stealing a horse for Holley if he sent him out this way, but he thought it still might be safer for Holley to go out this back trail on foot than to try to get through the guarded pass at the other end on horseback.

Finally Ridge paused on a small ledge, deciding that he must give up the exploration and go back. He turned and was surprised at the height he had attained in so short a time. The valley floor, at least 200 feet below, was spread out before him like a map, its features faintly identifiable in the moonlight.

Within half an hour he was back at the shed where Holley was tied. The light was out now and he listened at the wall a moment to make sure Maria was gone, then went inside. He struck a match and saw Holley, stretched out on the ground like a log. The look of dread on the young man's face was quickly replaced by hope and delight when he recognized Ridge Parkman.

Ridge shook the match out and then knelt beside Holley to remove the gag which Maria had replaced. "How you doin', ol' son?" Ridge asked as he helped his friend sit up. "Not so good right now, I reckon."

"Parkman, if I wasn't tied up right now," Billy said, "I'd hug your damn neck."

"Wal," Ridge drawled as he started to work on the knots at Billy's wrists, "I'm gonna untie you for a while, but you've got to promise to control yourself. We can't have no neck huggin' amongst marshals. But it is good to see you, too, Billy."

He untied Billy and the young man stretched his limbs weakly like a grandfather getting out of bed in the morning. Ridge found the lamp Maria had used and lit it, then set it behind a crate where only a faint amount of light shone out into the shed.

He surveyed Billy close up and said, "They've been workin' you over pretty good, haven't they?"

"It's been rough," Billy agreed, "but I reckon it's better'n what they give Mark."

"Yeah, I found him out there," Ridge said quietly. "That's how I ended up here."

"I got some gettin' even to do around here on that score," Billy hissed bitterly. "When we get outa here an' I get my hands on some guns, I'm gonna head back this way an' start drawin' blood."

"We'll get 'em all," Ridge promised. "Every last bastard that had anything to do with that."

"Good. Let's get goin' Ridge, 'fore somebody comes out here an' checks on me again." He started stiffly to his feet, but Ridge stopped him.

"Hold on a minute, Billy," he said. He dreaded having to tell his friend this after showing up so suddenly and promising him his freedom, but he had been carefully mulling over a plan in his head and had already decided how things had to be done.

Billy turned to Ridge curiously. Then Ridge went on. "I hate to have to say this, but you can't leave just yet. When we get done talkin', I'm goin' to tie you back up jus' the way I found you."

"The hell you are, Parkman!" Bill growled, his voice rising angrily before he caught himself.

"Now jus' wait a damn minute an' listen to what I got to say," Ridge ordered. "It'd be easy enough if we was both goin' out together, but we ain't. When I send you on your way, I'm stayin' here 'til I can take Blackie Crystal back with me." He quickly explained to the young man about the capture of Blackie and Mexican Joe, and about how they had been allowed to escape with Ridge's aid.

"When I send you outa here, I want to make sure you stay gone, an' I want to make sure you stay alive out there. That means you have to have food an' water an' a gun, which I ain't got on me right now an' don't exactly know how to get. When you go, you won't have no horse, so you'll have to make your way back to Adobe City on foot, an' I figger that's at least a week's walkin' for a stout man in the best of health, which you don't 'pear to be at the moment."

Billy had calmed down some and was now listening to Ridge closely as he outlined the plan he had worked out for Billy's escape.

When he finished, Ridge pulled out his pocket knife and opened the blade. "Put this somewhere where you can get to it after you're tied up again," Parkman said, "but remember. Don't try to make your break until full dark tomorrow. The supplies will be where I told you, I hope, an' if you follow my directions, you won't have no trouble findin' the trail out."

"Okay, Ridge," Billy conceded. "I'll do it the way you said. An' thanks . . . thanks for puttin' your neck on the block for me. It's a thing I won't forget I promise you."

Ridge reached out and solemnly shook Billy's hand before beginning to retie him. Finally he put out the lamp and moved to the door. Turning there, he said, "Good luck, friend," and then stepped out into the night.

It took Parkman only a few minutes to work his way back along the line of cabins to the main building, but as he was preparing to get past it and go down to his own cabin, he heard footsteps on the front porch. Cautiously he stepped into a shadow and waited. At the edge of the porch, Slim Bettermore paused to light a smoke, then stepped to the ground and started walking away. His friend Bill was close behind him.

Ridge realized that the two men were headed toward his cabin to wake him, and with a rush of anticipation he wondered what would happen when they got there and found him gone. As they started down in front of the row of cabins, Ridge hurried along on a course parallel to theirs, but behind the cabins.

When the two men reached the third cabin, Slim called out, "Parks. Let's go."

In a moment there came the sound of the door scraping open and Slim called out from inside to his partner, "He ain't in here."

"Where's he at, then?" Bill asked.

"How in the hell should I know?" Slim snapped. "I ain't his damn mother. Maybe he went over to Blackie's."

"There ain't no light in Blackie's cabin."

Ridge quickly unbuckled his belt, opened the top couple of buttons on his pants, and started around the cabin. When he neared Bill, he began fastening them up again.

"I was out back," Ridge explained. "I felt nature's callin'."

"Well, come on, Parks," Slim grumbled. "Them other guards get mad as hell when you come on late. Better take a coat out with you if you got one, too. Up there on them cliffs at night it gets cold as a heifer's teat in a Montana snowstorm."

"I'll take my blanket," Ridge said. He stepped inside the cabin and picked up his blanket and rifle before joining the two men out front.

As they walked down to the entrance to the valley and began climbing up to the guard positions high up on the rocks above, Slim told Ridge, "You ain't allowed to build no fires out here, but you can prob'ly get away with a smoke now'n again if you shelter the match.

"I'll take the head of the pass, an' you'll be in the middle. Bill'll be back here. Char told you 'bout who gets through an' who don't, an' if you hear me or Bill start shootin', you blast anything down there that you can rest your sights on."

"An' one other thing," Bill added. "Even if you gotta throw sand in your eyes to keep 'em open, don't go to sleep. Ol' Binnaker, he takes this guardin' stuff pretty serious, it bein' his valley an' all, an' sometimes he sneaks around at night sorta checkin' up. If he catches you sleepin' on guard duty . . ."

"He takes you to that damn everlovin' post of his, huh?" Ridge interrupted.

"He might jus' split your gizzard on the spot," Bill said dryly. "But if he don't, you'll be wishin' soon enough that he did."

"Suddenly I don't feel sleepy a'tall," Ridge announced.

Within a few minutes they were all in position. Slim was on the highest point of rock at the head of the pass, in the place where Ridge had first spotted the man with the field glasses when he and Blackie and Joe were riding in. In the daylight, a man up there had a clear view miles up and down the valley, as well as easy access to anybody trying to get by him in the pass below. Though their view was limited now by the nighttime darkness and their guarding was as much a matter of listening as it was of watching, it would still be difficult for anybody to get through the pass without being detected.

Ridge wished he had some way of informing Henry Lott about the layout of this place. Three men at these heights, armed with good repeating rifles, could spread a withering fire on any attacking force below them, but lives could probably be saved if Lott and his men knew beforehand what they would be running into. Leaving now was out of the question, though. Ridge had his orders, and they were to stay here until Billy Holley was safe and the prisoners who escaped from the Adobe City jail were either back in custody or dead. Lott and his forces would just have to find out for themselves.

Ridge hunkered down in a niche of rock, wrapped the blanket tightly about him to block the constant icy wind which swept

the summits where he was, and with stiff
fingers began to build the first of a countless number of cigarettes he would smoke
during the night.

CHAPTER SEVEN

The long hours of darkness passed slowly. Sometime midway through the shift a lone horseman rode through the pass below and into the valley. Ridge heard the *clop-clop* of the horse's hooves on the stones below, and later caught a glimpse of the shadowy, slouching figure passing by, but Slim let him go by unchallenged and so Ridge and Bill did the same.

The first light of morning over the mountains to the east was a welcome sight, and when the sun had risen high enough, Ridge moved from his sheltered hiding place out into the warm sunlight. But it was still nearly three hours before anybody showed up to relieve him. Ridge nodded tiredly to his replacement and then started down the trail toward the cabins without waiting for Slim. When he reached the place where Bill had been, another man was there and Bill was far ahead on the pathway.

Instead of returning to his cabin and passing out on the cot as he would have liked, Ridge went to the main building and ordered himself coffee and a big breakfast. There would be time for rest later, but right then he had some things to do. He had been thinking about the situation all night and had finally worked out the skeleton of a plan in his mind.

Char Binnaker came over, carrying two mugs of steaming black coffee, and sat down at the table with Ridge. "Anything go on out there last night?" he asked.

"One rider came through," Ridge told him. "But guess you know that."

"Yeah, I saw him," Binnaker said. "I jus' wanted to make sure you did, too." He paused for a moment to take a gulp of the coffee and then went on. "He's a small-time holdup man from over your way. Maybe you know him. Name's Brody McDonald."

Ridge paused in mid bite and looked up at Binnaker. He knew McDonald all right. He had arrested him two years before and started him on his way to Leavenworth Prison. Ridge thrust another forkful of meat in his mouth and chewed on it as Binnaker watched him closely. This was a critical moment, Ridge knew, and he was going to have to say and do just the right thing if he wanted to get through it.

"Where's he at?" Ridge finally asked.

Binnaker motioned toward the row of cabins on the west side with his thumb and said, "Fourth one down. Sleepin'. You do know him, huh?"

"I know him," Ridge said coldly. Then he looked Binnaker square in the eye and asked, "You allow killin' in this place, or do I have to haul his carcass out of here to do it?"

"This is a rough place," Binnaker said. "Men fightin' an' dyin' 'round here all the time, but it don't make me no nevermind since this place is only full of no-count sonsofbitches anyhow. You kill 'im fair, an' I get his outfit an' poke. Okay?"

"I don't care what happens to his stuff," Ridge said. "It's just his life I want. You gonna tell him I'm here? He'll backshoot me sure as hell if you do."

"What's between you an' him is your business," Binnaker said indifferently. "I ain't tellin' 'im nothin'." He got up to leave, but Ridge stopped him.

"Where's Maria this mornin'?"

Binnaker turned with a crooked half-grin and said, " 'Pears like you'd be too tired after spendin' the night on the cliffs."

"I got a notion to get tireder," Ridge

grinned back. "Where's she at?"

"She jus' got back a little while ago," Binnaker said. "She's upstairs."

Ridge pulled out a double eagle and put it on the table. "How long'll that make her my woman for?" he asked.

Binnaker snatched up the gold piece and quickly pocketed it. "I'll tell you when to stop," he said. Then he turned to the Indian woman behind the bar and said, "Go get Maria an' tell her to haul her ass down to Parks's cabin. Tell her she's his 'til I say different."

The Mexican woman was waiting for Ridge when he returned to his cabin. As he stepped through the door she looked a little guilty and he guessed that she had probably been searching the place for some hidden stash of money or valuables, but he let that go by because he had not left anything of value there.

"Hello, Maria," Ridge said, tossing his blanket on the bed and leaning his rifle in a corner.

"You buy Maria?" she asked, curious about why he would do such a thing.

"That's right," Ridge said. "I gave Binnaker twenty dollars for you an' I want you to stay with me all the time. You understand?"

She smiled suddenly and said, "Maybe you get well, eh, *señor?*"

"No, it's not that," Ridge chuckled. He went over to the bed and sat down on the bunk, then motioned for her to sit beside him. "You an' me," he told her quietly, "are goin' to help Holley get away."

"No, no!" she said, shaking her head quickly as a look of abject fear came over her face. She rose and started to the door, but Ridge stood up behind her and caught her arm. He cuffed her across the face with his open hand, knocking her to the floor. Then he quickly drew his revolver and pointed it at her head. He hated to use this kind of tactics on a woman, even this kind of woman, but he knew it was the reasoning she would most easily understand.

Maria's dark Latin eyes were as big as half dollars as she stared at the deadly barrel of the Colt. She was shaking uncontrollably and whimpering slightly, muttering either prayers or pleas in her native tongue. Ridge stood waiting for a moment, letting the fear engulf her and soak deep into the fiber of her being. He would kill her if it became absolutely necessary, and he wanted her to realize that fact with crystal clarity.

Then finally he knelt beside her and told her quietly, "If you try to leave me, I'll blow your head off right now an' tell Binnaker you tried to rob me. You savvy that, Maria?" She nodded her head, speechless as she stared in horror at the barrel of the pistol.

Ridge stood up, holstered the revolver and, putting a hand under Maria's arm, helped her gently to her feet. He led her over to the bed and they sat back down, then he said, "Now. Let's start over. Let me ask you something. Do you like Holley?"

"*Si.* He is nice boy. Poor Holley."

"Right. Poor Holley. Do you know what they are planning to do to him tonight?"

"Kill him, *señor.* Cut him with the knife."

"Wal, he's an *amigo* of mine an' I don't intend to let nobody take a blade to his hide long as I can do somethin' to stop it. I know a way we can save him an' nobody will know it was us that did it. Binnaker will know you were with me an' he won't think you helped Holley escape. Do you understand that?"

She nodded yes, but her eyes were still skeptical and afraid. Ridge could imagine the horrible position Maria now found herself in. On the one hand, Ridge had promised to kill her if she did not help him with his escape plans, and on the other there was the awesome wrath of Char Binnaker to be faced if he learned that she was a part of the plot. She had probably tasted the fruits of Binnaker's anger before and knew how terrible they could be, and even if she had not, she had surely seen him torture and kill enough other people to know the atrocities he was capable of. Ridge tried to calm her fears with quiet words and reassurances.

"If you stay with me all day, who will take food and water out to Holley today?"

"Maybe another girl. Maybe Indian bitch."

"An' if you don't see Holley all day, an' then he escapes tonight, who will Binnaker blame for him getting away?"

"Indian bitch!" Maria exclaimed. At last the light of hope and interest shone in her eyes as she understood Ridge's reasoning.

"That's right," Ridge said, sharing the happy moment of revelation with her. "Now, if you do everything right, when I leave here, I'll take you away with me to someplace safe, someplace better than this. Would you like that? Will you help?"

"You take me go from here?" she asked, scarcely able to believe she had heard him correctly.

"That's right."

"Yes, yes! I help you, cowboy," she said with excitement, reaching out spontaneously and giving him a long hug.

"Okay, that's good," Ridge said when he was able to break her grip on his neck. "If you tell anybody else about this, or if you don't do something I tell you, you get this." He patted the revolver on his hip. "Or maybe I'll tell Binnaker you tried to set Holley loose."

"No, I help! I help!" Maria insisted urgently. "I like you. I like Holley. I like go away. I help."

"Let's get some sleep then, an' I'll tell you more later," Ridge said, rising and unbuckling his gunbelt before dropping down on the bunk. Then, despite the fact that there were other bunks in the cabin, Maria curled up on the floor beside Ridge's bed like a faithful dog. She closed her eyes and was almost immediately asleep.

But Ridge lay awake for a while, gazing down at this strange, abused woman who had suddenly become his ally. It was curious, he thought, this apparent devotion to him so soon after he had threatened her life and forced her into doing something which she absolutely did not want to do. It said a lot about the life she must have led, about the men who had ruled her existence in the past. In a way, he thought, being dominated with a combination of terror and occasional warmth was probably the only kind of existence she had ever known, and perhaps it represented security to her.

She was a striking contradiction to the spirited and genteel Rosalie Holley. Though it already seemed like a month, it had been only a couple of days since he had stood out there on a hill at the edge of Adobe City and shared a kiss with Rosalie. He wondered how she would react if she saw him now, in a bunk with his filthy Mexican whore, the woman he had bought half an hour earlier with a double eagle, lying on the floor beside him. She would not understand, of course; she could not be expected to comprehend this kind of life and this level of society.

But, Ridge thought with a sudden feeling of wistful discontent, he did understand them. He well knew the Binnakers and Blackies and Marias in this world, the killers and criminals and people who lived without pride or purpose — the dregs. A man with the kind of job Parkman had fought to protect the respectable element of society, but still he was an outsider, seldom among them. More often he was in the dives and brothels, the bandit camps and wilderness hideouts, because to deal with criminals he had to wallow with them on their own terms, to share their gutters.

But still he never became like them. The strong purpose in his life, the overriding motivation of his law man's profession kept him going, kept his mind and morals above this kind of people even when he was in the midst of them. This kind of place and these kinds of people had never infected him with the disease of evil which rotted their souls and wasted their lives.

He tossed and turned on the cot for a while, tired but unable to sleep. But finally he forced his mind away from the present, off the staggering tasks he had ahead of him, and played his personal game of considering the creature comforts which awaited him when the job was done. Soon he was asleep.

They woke about noon and Ridge gave Maria some money to go up to the kitchen and get some food. He instructed her to get only bread and meat, as much as they would let her have for the money, and to also bring an empty flour or potato sack back with her. If asked, she was to explain that he did not have any saddlebags and needed the cloth sack to keep his personal belongings in.

When she was gone, Ridge went over near the window where the light was best, spread his blanket out on the floor, and began disassembling his revolver. A thin coat of dust and grit had collected on all the oiled parts and he began to wipe them clean with a piece of cloth. The gun lay in pieces in front of him when Maria returned with two tin plates heaped with food.

She sat down on the bed and was about to start eating, but Ridge stopped her. "No, don't eat that," he said. "We're going to save it, an' then do the same thing with what you get for supper later on. Today you an' I do without food."

Maria looked confused and saddened by the prospect of a day-long fast, but she set the plates of food on the bed and left them alone.

Ridge took one small piece of meat from a plate and carried it back over to the window. Lacking any sort of gun oil, he used small amounts of the grease from the meat to oil the critical parts of the gun. It would have to be removed later and the parts lubricated properly, but right then he needed a clean gun in good working order and that was the best he could do for lubrication.

When he finished reassembling and holstering the Colt, he went back over to the food. Tearing strips from his blanket, he wrapped the bread and meat separately, then thrust all the small bundles into the sack. He searched the small cabin thoroughly and finally found a hiding place for the sack in a niche up among the thick-hewn beams which supported the roof.

Maria watched all of this with brows knit in confusion. "It's food for Holley," Ridge explained at last. "When he leaves, he'll have a long walk ahead of him an' he'll need somethin' to eat out there in the mountains. An' he'll need water, too. Can't count on him comin' across some regular enough. Do you think you could get some sort of canteen or water skin for him?"

Maria thought for a moment and then suggested, "Maybe whiskey bottle."

"Sure. That would be fine. The first chance you get, bring two or three whiskey bottles full of water back here. But be careful about it. If anybody sees us gathering up all this truck, they'll start getting suspicious."

"At siesta time," Maria said. "Everybody asleep and not see Maria."

"That's good," Ridge told her. He paused for a moment and then said, "Now, there's just one more thing we need for Holley. A gun. Does Binnaker keep a lot of guns in the big house?"

"*Si.* He have many guns. In every room."

"Is there any in the kitchen near the back door? What we need is a rifle if you can get your hands on one."

"One is there."

"An' ammunition? Maybe a couple of boxes?"

"Si."

"Okay, Maria. The next time you go up there, you make sure that rifle an' the cartridges are still in the kitchen, but you leave them alone for now."

Ridge quit talking when he heard footsteps approaching on the gravel outside. He went over to the doorway and saw Blackie Crystal approaching the cabin.

"Ain't interruptin' nothin', am I?" he asked with a knowing chuckle.

"Not right now," Ridge grinned.

"Good," Blackie said. "I want you to come up an' have a drink with me."

"Sure," Ridge said. He turned back to Maria and told her gruffly, "You stay here, woman. I'll be back later." Then he joined Blackie outside and they started away toward the main building.

"Char said you bought that fat Mex woman full-time," Blackie commented. "I didn't know you had that kind of *dinero* to throw around. Gotta admit, though. I had her last night an' she's fair, 'cept for that gawdawful stink."

"I ain't got much money," Ridge said. "Jus' the chicken scratch I stole in Three Pines, but I figger I might as well enjoy what I got."

"Yeah," Blackie chuckled. "You'll have money soon enough. We'll be plannin' another big job soon as I send my scouts put. I figger to hit a small town next time, maybe a mining camp payroll or an ore shipment."

"Sounds good to me," Ridge said. "There wouldn't be as much law around then to light out after us when the job's done."

"It's the way I see it," Blackie agreed. "I think maybe I got too ambitious with the Adobe City bank job, an' it almost cost me my neck. We jus' got used to easy pickin's down in Texas. Them little settlements we raided never had no more'n one ol' worn-out tin star or two, an' when the big guns did get after us, alls we had to do was hightail it back across the border into Mexico where they couldn't follow."

They reached the main building and entered together. The place was empty except for Binnaker, who poured drinks for them when they walked over to the bar. Then as they resumed their conversation, the big landlord went back to his chair at the end of the bar where he sat mending a damaged bridle.

"What happened to your setup down there in Texas?" Ridge asked.

"It was the damnedest thing," Blackie said. "One day the Texas Rangers got on our trail, an' when we got to the Rio Grande River, they jus' kept comin' like they didn't know they was crossin' into another country. They dogged us like a pack of starvin' wolves for three days, 'til me an' the men couldn't go no farther. We turned an' fought then, but it was pure slaughter. I never seen no bunch of fightin' men like them Rangers. Man, if I had me thirty, maybe forty men like that in my gang . . ."

"I ain't never tangled with no Rangers, but I've heard they're tough."

"Tough is right," Blackie agreed. "I had thirty-two men when they got on our tails, but there wasn't but a dozen of us got away. Wouldn't of been that many if I hadn't had Joe along. He knew the country an' he led us out of there all right.

"By then I'd seen them Rangers was out after my hide, an' I decided there wasn't nothin' to do but get the hell clean outa that part of the country. So we come up here to Colorado. There's always money to be made in the goldfields."

Ridge scarcely glanced around when another man came in and took a seat at a table in one corner. Binnaker went over and took his order, then crossed back behind the bar and went in the kitchen. In a moment he came back out with a plate of food, drew a beer from a keg behind the bar, and carried both over to the newcomer. As he set the plate and mug on the table, he said, "I'll be takin' my money now, McDonald. Four bucks, includin' the cabin for the night."

"Hell, I'll be here awhile," the man complained. "Jus' keep it on account. I got money enough."

"I'll be takin' it now," Binnaker repeated in a voice which left no room for argument.

Ridge tensed when he heard Binnaker mention the man's name. He had for the moment completely forgotten about Brody McDonald and the problem that his presence here posed, but now, suddenly, the time had come for him to deal with it. Blackie had been talking, but quieted when he noticed the abrupt change on Ridge's features. "What's the matter, Parks?" he asked, but Ridge ignored him.

When Char Binnaker left Brody McDonald's table, Ridge turned slowly until he faced the middle of the room, his right hand down near his revolver and his eyes fixed on the man at the table.

McDonald was a beanpole of a man with an incredibly ugly, stupid-looking face, and yet there was a look of shifty cunning in his darting, cautious eyes. He was using his fingers to cram huge amounts of food into his mouth, then washing it down with gulping draughts of beer. He ate like a man who had been raised in a pig lot, smacking and chomping and pausing occasionally to wipe his greasy hands on his equally grimy shirt front.

Ridge just stared at the man for a moment. He had no particular liking for McDonald, but now he felt a rush of pity for him. For an instant he tried to come up with some other possible way to handle this situation. But there was none. It was just McDonald's misfortune that he had picked this particular time to seek the refuge of The Havens, but now that he was here, his presence was a clear danger to the lives of both Parkman and Billy Dean Holley. It had been two years since their last encounter, and it was possible that he might not recognize Parkman, especially in this unlikely place, but Ridge could not take that chance.

Parkman took two deep breaths, spread his feet apart a little more, and checked with his fingers to make sure the leather strap was loose from the hammer of his revolver and back out of the way. Then he said, "Mc-Donald! Get up an' go for it!"

The expression on McDonald's face when he looked up at Parkman was one of complete shock and a great amount of fear. Probably he still did not recognize the law man and had no idea why he was so suddenly being called to account, but from the flash of terror which momentarily twisted his features deep within him, he seemed to realize that the time of his death was at hand. Instinctively, his hand sought his revolver as he started to stand up.

Ridge drew and fired three quick shots, fanning the hammer with the heel of his left hand as his right hand kept the pistol trained on his victim. In the confined space, the roar of the gun was like an explosion, and immediately the room filled with thick smoke.

McDonald tumbled backwards across the chair he had been sitting in, then rolled sideways and ended up face down on the floor. As quiet returned, the breeze from the windows began to thin the cloud of smoke and push it out the front door.

Ridge just stood there, his revolver still in his hand. As the smoke cleared, he shifted his glance across the room to Binnaker, meeting his eyes with a stern direct gaze, then looking over to the surprised Blackie Crystal.

"Well, I'll be damned!" Blackie muttered. "Parks, you're one cold sonofabitch, ain't you?"

"Me an' him had to settle this," Ridge said. "We couldn't both of us stay in this place . . . not alive anyhow."

"Woman," Binnaker shouted. When his squaw came through the doorway from the kitchen, he nodded toward the body of the dead man on the floor and said, "Take care of that."

Silently, as if she had been ordered to clean up nothing worse than a spilled plate of food, the Indian woman went over to the body of the dead man. She moved the table aside, then picked up one of his feet and began tugging at his boot. Within a couple of minutes, she had stripped off his boots, trousers, gunbelt, and hat. His shirt was such a bloody mess that she didn't try to save that. She carried the dead man's things into the back of the building and then returned and began struggling to drag the body out the front door. None of the men offered to help, but she eventually got it done alone, leaving a wide trail of blood across the room.

Blackie Crystal was impressed, even pleased, by the killing. "Parks, you cold sonofabitch," he repeated, slapping Ridge on the shoulder and pushing a glass of whiskey in front of him.

Parkman considered making up some lie to explain why he had killed McDonald so suddenly, but then decided to just leave it all a mystery. Neither Char Binnaker nor Blackie Crystal seemed to have any trouble accepting the fact that Brody McDonald had done Ridge some deadly wrong, and that was enough.

Ridge gulped the drink down quickly and poured another, hoping to calm the rush of nervous tension which he knew would soon flood through him. It was generally that way after he had to kill a man. During the act, he almost felt as if his thoughts and nerves went dead, leaving only unfeeling, calculating instinct to do what had to be done. But later it generally came back in a flood, sometimes making his hands tremble violently and his body quiver in spasms. It was an ugly thing to take a life, no matter how just the reason.

"Did you know you was goin' to kill that man when we was comin' over here?" Blackie asked.

"I knew he was in camp an' that I had to do it sooner or later."

"An' you jus' let me go on jawin' away about the job. Hell, why didn't you say somethin'? I woulda helped you."

"I didn't need no help, Blackie," Ridge said, finally mustering a grin.

"No, it don't look like you did at that," Blackie grinned back at him.

"Let's talk 'bout somethin' else, okay?" Ridge asked. "Let's talk 'bout the job an' how much we're goin' to make."

"Sure, sure," Blackie agreed. "An with that gun of yours, I guarantee it'll be plenty. Char, bring us another bottle."

He talked on while Ridge watched the Indian woman outside lead a horse up to the porch and begin tying a rope around Brody McDonald's bootless feet.

CHAPTER EIGHT

It promised to be quite a fete, thanks to the liberal spending of Blackie Crystal. He had bought an entire steer from the small herd which Char Binnaker kept in the valley, and had it slaughtered and quartered early in the afternoon. Char's squaw and another woman who lived in the camp built huge fires in two open pits in front of the big house, and then muscled the large quarters of beef onto spits over them.

By midafternoon others in the camp began drifting up toward the big house to join Ridge and Blackie at the bar there, but today no money changed hands. Blackie was paying for everything. It was no wonder, Ridge thought, that the large sums of money such as the $14,000 they took from that Adobe City bank did not last the gang very long. He was also willing to bet that, though Blackie and his men were the star boarders right now, when the money from the bank job was all spent, Binnaker would be quick enough to tell them to either pull another job or pull their stakes and ride out.

But what disgusted Ridge Parkman the most was the underlying reason for the festivities. This was a marshal-killing party. Blackie had decreed that sometime after dark, after everybody had eaten and drunk their fill, the prisoner would be brought forth, and his death was to be the highlight of the evening's entertainment.

Ridge stayed up at the big house for a couple of hours, drinking and laughing with the others, but he did not want to stay too long or drink too much. He had to be in reasonably good shape later in case anything went wrong with his plan and he had to make some quick changes.

Maria was still waiting in the cabin when he returned. She seemed bored and was glad that he had come back, but she was also worried.

"Cowboy, you okay?" she asked as he came in the door.

"Sure, Maria. I'm fine."

"Rosa tell me you shoot the man," Maria said. "You do this?"

"Yeah, I did. He was an ol' enemy that jus' had the bad luck to show up while I was here." He went over and sat down on

137

the bed, then asked, "You hungry, Maria?"

"Yes, yes," she said eagerly. "Very hungry."

"Good," Ridge told her. "So am I. Why don't you get some food. Lots of meat an' lots of bread, but don't eat any of it. Okay?"

Maria put on a pouting look which made Ridge laugh, but then he told her, "Don't worry. I ain't plannin' to starve you to death. You can eat your fill tonight at Blackie's party."

When she was gone, Ridge reached up to the beam to make sure the bag of food was still there. On the beam beside the bag he felt three bottles laid side by side and knew that sometime while he was gone, Maria had been able to sneak up and secure Holley's water supply.

The woman was soon back with more food, and again Ridge carefully wrapped it and put it in the bag. Then he wrapped each water bottle separately and put them in the bag, and as an afterthought, dropped in his bag of tobacco and papers, as well as a handful of matches. Then he stuck the bag far up under his cot and pushed his blanket in to hide it.

"That's that, I guess," Ridge said, standing up.

"What we do now?" Maria asked, her eyes gazing up at Ridge wistfully. "Damn war.

138

What we do now, cowboy?"

"Do you have a pretty dress, Maria?" Ridge asked. "Something pretty to wear to a surprise party for Blackie? When we go out there tonight, I want to be with the best-looking woman in camp."

"*Si, si.* I have a dress," Maria said with enthusiasm. "I wear for my cowboy, okay?"

"Yeah, but first why don't you take a bath? You go up an' wash an' put on your pretty dress, an' then you come back an' get me. Then we'll go to the party."

Maria gave him a quick excited kiss and then ran out of the cabin, happy as a child on the last day of school.

Ridge pulled off his boots and lay back on the bunk. So far so good, he thought

He scarcely recognized the woman who came into the cabin about sunset and woke him with a light touch on the hand. Her dark skin was shiny clean and her long black hair, washed and brushed, fell in shimmering waves across her shoulders and down her back. The red silky dress she wore was faded and straining at its seams across her bosom and around her waist, but it was still a pleasing change from the shapeless, filthy frock she usually wore. It was obviously one of the last souvenirs of better, and thinner, days for Maria.

"You look great, Maria," Ridge said as he sat up and looked her over. His compliment was sincere. She looked years younger and much more pretty than she had when she left the cabin an hour or so earlier, and it seemed to him that he could almost picture the beautiful young woman she had been before hard living had begun to ravage her body and soul.

"I save this dress for a special time," Maria said with a smile. "For a special man." She stared down at Ridge with an unmistakable look of adoration which he nervously ignored. He could understand how she was beginning to feel. He was probably the first man in years who had treated her like a human being, let alone been kind to her and paid her compliments, but this was no time to let any emotions or affections get in the way. There was still work to be done.

It was nearly dark by the time he and Maria readied the gathering. Everybody in camp seemed to be there, gathered around a large bonfire the women had built. Ridge took a quick head count and decided that nobody was missing except the three men who were undoubtedly on guard at the pass. That was what he wanted, for everybody to be in one place where he could keep an eye on them.

Timing was going to be critical now. All the steps of his plan had to be carried out in darkness, but he did not want to wait too long after dark for fear that Blackie and Mexican Joe might decide it was time to bring out the guest of honor. Ridge figured that Billy Holley would need at least an hour's head start before he stood any chance of making his escape last. He would be weak from the long imprisonment and starting out in the dark on an unknown trail, and the chances were that Char Binnaker knew every rock and gulch in the country surrounding his domain.

But that did not mean that Holley would be nothing more than a desperate hunted man out there. Even though he was young, Billy was wise in the ways of these mountains — he knew how to track, hide, and fight with the best of them, having studied the marshal's trade under the excellent guidance of Henry Lott. If Binnaker, Blackie, and the rest got too hot after him, it was likely that Billy would be able to work out a few desperate surprises to spring on them.

The delicious odor of the roasting beef filled the air around the big bonfire, and Maria immediately went over and began helping the other women tend to the big quarters of beef. Two wooden crates of whiskey bottles sat on the ground near where the men were gathered, and Ridge took one of the bottles and stopped at the edge of the group.

Blackie was in the midst of a retelling of the shooting of Brody McDonald and when he saw Ridge approach, he called out, "Here he is, boys. Our new gunslinger."

Ridge pulled the stopper from the bottle and took a healthy slug, then glanced around the group with a whiskey-primed grin on his face. He recognized only a few of the men, but Blackie did not bother with any introductions before launching back into his tale.

"I didn't know what the hell was goin' on," Crystal said, "but all of a sudden ol' Parks here got this cold damn glint in his eye. Then he spun 'round an' squared off with that feller. That McDonald, he never knew what hit him. Jus' 'bam, bam' an' he was on his way to hell."

"What'd he do to you, Parks?" one of the men in the group asked Ridge.

"It was a long time ago," Ridge said, taking another hit on the bottle to give himself a moment to think. "Me an' Brody met in a bar in Wichita an' come up with this scam

142

to rustle us some cattle thereabouts, and then to sell 'em to a trail herd that needed a few head to round out their contract quota. When we got the steers, I stayed with 'em in this little gulch while he went out to find a buyer. But he run into trouble an' so he jus' skipped. The rancher we took 'em from got on our trail an' damn near caught me, an' me jus' sittin' there like a damn fool waitin' for Brody to come back."

Everybody nodded their heads, agreeing that it was a killing offense, and Blackie put his stamp of approval on the act by saying, "Bet he's wishin' right now he'd been more square."

"I don't care what he's wishin' now," Ridge mumbled. "I know I got my wish."

The talk soon turned to other old grudges and shootouts, but Ridge took very little part in it. He sat around on the edge of the group, pulling on the bottle occasionally for show and doing his best to keep his eyes on the comings and goings of everybody. He watched with approval as the small tack shed near the corrals slowly grew faint and finally disappeared in the growing darkness. Only occasionally did the licking flames of the bonfire throw out enough light, for him to catch a glimpse of the building where Holley was imprisoned.

When he saw Maria coming toward him with a big slab of meat and some bread on a tin plate, he stepped away from the group and went to meet her.

As he took the plate from the woman, he said quietly to her, "It's time, Maria. Everybody's getting drunk now an' they won't notice if you're gone for a little while. Go back to the cabin an' get the bag of food, then stop by the kitchen for that rifle an' ammo. Take 'em out an' put 'em on the far side of the tack shed, an' then get back here quick as you can. Don't even stop to talk to Holley. He knows where to look for the stuff an' he'll hear you leave it for him. Okay?"

Maria did not look happy about her mission, but she nodded her understanding and started away. She headed around the side of the big house in the general direction of the outhouses behind it, and Ridge carried his plate and bottle back to the fringes of the group of men.

The men were getting drunk and rowdy now, making regular trips over to the smoke-blackened carcass over the fire and chasing the whores playfully around the clearing. As Ridge took his first bite of the charred meat, he glanced around, trying to see if anybody had noticed him and Maria talking or had paid attention to her leaving.

144

The rest of the group continued to laugh and talk, but across the fire Ridge spotted the small dark eyes of Mexican Joe Rodriguez watching him. The firelight danced in the Mexican's eyes, and though he held a plate of food and had a bottle sitting beside him on the ground, he was doing nothing at the moment but staring at Ridge.

Ridge returned the cold look for a moment, gnawing the hunk of meat hungrily as he tried to convey the message that he would not tolerate any trouble from the Mexican. Joe, he knew, would become doubly cautious now that Ridge had showed his prowess and become one of Blackie's favorites by killing Brody McDonald, but he still had the feeling that the Mexican had not forgotten or forgiven the beating Ridge gave him in jail. So far he and Joe had successfully avoided each other here in The Havens and their big confrontation had not come yet, but it was still a score yet to be settled.

Finally Ridge glanced away, and immediately his eyes caught the movement of a shadowy form near the tack shed. It was little more than a flicker of light against dark as a flame of the fire licked up and threw some light in that direction, but it was enough to make Ridge nervous for a moment. If anyone else saw that, Ridge knew, the party could become violent in an instant.

But nobody sounded the alarm and in a moment Maria was back, buttoning up the front of her dress as she rounded the corner of the big house. It was a nice touch. One outlaw, staggering away from the fire to relieve himself, caught the Mexican woman up in his arms briefly, lifting her clear off the ground and twirling her around in a spin which nearly carried both of them to the ground. Maria gave him a quick kiss on the mouth and then skillfully twisted out of his arms before coming on.

When she reached Ridge, she took the bottle from him and gulped down an amazing draught of the whiskey, then smiled up at him and said, "It's all done."

Ridge could still feel the penetrating eyes of Mexican Joe on him and he did not want it to appear that he and Maria were exchanging secrets, so he wrapped an arm around her and gave her a long drunken kiss, then sent her back to get him more food.

Now that the deed was done and Holley was safely on his way, Ridge allowed himself to relax some. It would be a simple thing now for him and Maria to stay together and in the midst of the party, thus cinching; their alibi when it was finally discovered that the captive marshal had escaped.

He led the woman a small distance apart, but still within easy sight of everyone, and they sat down on the ground close together. He paid her a lot of attention now, both for appearance's sake and to show her his appreciation for what she had done.

But soon he began to view as a warning signal the warm surge of desire he was beginning to feel for the sad, oppressed woman. That meant he was getting too drunk, that his guard was dropping too low, and he refused the bottle when Maria took a turn at it and held it out to him. He stretched back on the ground and Maria lay beside him, her head on his shoulder and her hand on his chest.

"Jus' stay with me an' don't leave again for any reason," he told her quietly.

"I am happy here," Maria said. "That cowboy want me to go inside with him, but I tell him I am Parks' woman. Full time."

"I'm gonna keep my promise to you, Maria," Ridge vowed. " 'Fore this is over, I'm gonna get you out of here an' set you up somewhere with a job. But right now we jus' have to wait 'til they find out Holley's gone, an' then weather out what comes after. I don't know what's goin' to happen, but if I get in any trouble, you get away from me an' stay clear. Okay? I won't tell them you had anything to do with Holley's escape, an' you deny knowin' anything about it."

"I lie like hell," she laughed lightly and a little drunkenly from beside him, her face half buried in the haven of his shirt.

They stayed like that for a while as the party continued on without them. Finally, after at least another hour, Ridge saw Blackie, Binnaker, and Mexican Joe gather for a conference. He could not hear what they were talking about, but it was not hard to guess. Then in a moment Joe got another man and they started away toward the tack shed. At the same time, Binnaker went inside and brought out a length of rope, a thick teamster's bullwhip, and his long sheath knife. He carried them over and laid them on the ground near his dreaded punishment post.

Ridge and Maria sat up then as the crowd of people began to migrate in the direction of the post, the conversation as excited as a town expecting a circus.

It was only a moment before the man who had gone with Joe came running back toward the fire shouting, "He's gone,

Blackie! He got away!"

A few of the men grabbed up burning sticks from the fire and everyone began hurrying toward the tack shed. Mexican Joe had already lit the lamp there and was outside with it examining the ground around the shed. Blackie walked up to him and asked, "What the hell happened, Joe? Where'd he go?"

"I don't know," Joe said, his eyes still on the ground looking for clues. "Even the ropes are gone, and I don't find a trail yet."

That was smart, Ridge thought. Holley had taken the ropes with him so that nobody could see that they were cut and know he had been helped in his escape.

In a minute Char Binnaker showed up, carrying a large kerosene lamp, which lit up the whole area brightly. He immediately took charge of the situation. "Two of you men," he said, pointing to the two nearest him, "run down an' tell the guards what's happened. Some others of you get a count on these horses an' see if he got one. I don't think he could get outa here on horseback, but he might be fool enough to try."

Binnaker stepped inside the shed briefly with Blackie to look around, and when they came back out, he said, "Some of you go back an' start searchin' the buildings, an' the rest of you fan out an' start walkin' this way. There's an old trail up the backside of the valley that he might find. But don't nobody stray too far from the pack. We don't want him jumpin' somebody an' gettin' his hands on a gun."

Ridge joined the others as they began the search back in the direction of the hidden trail. When they reached the crack in the rock which Ridge had discovered the day before, Binnaker held the others back as he and Mexican Joe went forward to examine the ground. In a moment Binnaker turned his head back and said, "He come this way. He's on foot, too. Couldn't no horse make it up this trail."

"Where does that trail lead to?" Blackie asked.

"It goes right straight up the mountain," Binnaker said. "Up top he has a choice. He could either start down the other side, or go one way or t'other along the ridge."

"Anyway we could circle 'round an' head him off on horseback? He's bound to light out on the shortest route toward Adobe City. He ain't got no food, nor any water neither, so he'll need to get to them things as quick as he can."

Ridge quietly enjoyed the moment. Billy Dean Holly had a decent supply of both food and water, as well as a gun, and Ridge knew that would give him the ability to avoid doing anything predictable. He would figure out what they expected him to do, and then do something entirely different.

"Only a danged empty-headed moron would saddle up an' go ridin' out into these mountains at night," Binnaker said. "We could follow on foot, but it'd be such slow goin' that we never would have a hope in hell of catchin' up to him. I say we wait 'til mornin' an' then go 'round on horseback. We can break up into groups an' see if we can't pick up some sign of which way he went. Hell, it's a five- or six-day walk back to Adobe City, an' he oughta be weak as a kitten after the time he spent here."

Deprived of his enjoyment, Mexican Joe was quietly seething about the escape. He had been silent during the search, but now he spoke up to nobody in particular. "Maybe somebody help him get away," he said.

"Maybe so," Binnaker said. "But who would want to? The men that come here ain't exactly fond of no federal marshals."

"Maybe somebody here lies to us," the Mexican said.

"If you know somethin', Joe," Blackie said angrily, "then quit playin' this stupid guessin' game an' spit it out."

Ridge saw what was coming and decided to get a step ahead of the Mexican. "I did it," he said suddenly, taking a couple of steps forward into the lamplight. "Damn your hide, that's what you think, ain't it Rodriguez? Wal, you jus' go ahead an' spit it out like Blackie says, an' in a minute I'll fix it so you'll be spittin' up blood."

In an instant the Mexican squared off and the two men were ready to draw.

"Now jus' hold it a damn minute here, you two," Blackie said, stepping forward between them. "Is that it, Joe? You think that Parks let the marshal loose?"

The Mexican stared on but said nothing.

"Sure it was me, Blackie," Ridge said derisively. "I'm one of them damn marshals myself an' you're all under arrest"

Blackie ignored his taunts, turning to the Mexican and saying, "You're jus' mad 'cause he bested you back there in that jail, but don't forget he jumped that jailer an' got our asses out of there, too." Then, turning to Ridge, he said, "An' you listen here, Parks. I can see you an' the Mex is gonna have to settle this, but now ain't no time for a reckonin'. We got us other business to take care of first. I want that damn marshal."

"The time's comin', Blackie," Ridge said

bitterly. "An' it ain't far off."

"When we catch the marshal," Blackie promised. "After that, we find out if I get myself a new *segundo* or keep the same one I got."

Chapter Nine

When Ridge finally returned to his cabin a couple of hours later, Maria was not there. The door was ajar, and though he thought the men who had searched the buildings earlier had probably left it that way, he still entered the dark interior warily. That business with Mexican Joe was quickly coming to a head, and Ridge knew now that he was going to have to be especially careful every minute. Some men, even a lot of outlaws, considered it the proper thing to give an opponent a fair chance in a fight, but Ridge had Joe figured as the kind of scoundrel who would take his kills any way he could get them. A bullet in the back made a man just as dead as one in the front.

In a way he wished he could have gone ahead and forced a shootout with the Mexican out there when they had their confrontation. At least then it would be settled. He had enough on his mind already without having to watch every shadow and bush to make sure his antagonist was not lurking nearby, and he had no serious delusions about being able to take Mexican Joe back alive. Though daring, Blackie Crystal was crafty enough to give up if he was cornered, hoping for a chance to escape later, but Ridge thought Mexican Joe Rodriguez was too much of an impulsive maniac to ever submit to capture again, especially to Rich Parks, his enemy.

But despite the recent trouble, he still felt good. Half of his mission had been accomplished, and he had succeeded in engineering Holley's escape without revealing his true identity. Now he had to figure out a good way to take care of the second task Henry Lott had assigned him. Though he accepted the fact that he would likely kill the Mexican soon, he still hoped to take Blackie Crystal back to face trial and a legal hanging.

That was a process of the law which Parkman believed should be allowed to run its full course whenever it was possible. Killing outlaws in the field eliminated the problems and risks of taking them back, and it sure put an end to their criminal careers, but Parkman knew that it could not go on that way forever. As a law man, he liked to believe that he was something more than just a violent man who hunted down and killed other violent men. He hoped that someday enough of the Blackie Crystals would have been eliminated that no more Ridge Parkmans would be needed either.

He secured the cabin as best he could, fastening the shutters of the windows and forcing the door closed. Then he pulled off his boots and clothes and piled down on the bunk, pulling the shortened blanket over him.

He had almost drifted off into sleep when the noise began. At first he heard a dreadful wailing, the pitiful sound of a woman pleading or grieving in some strange tongue. Then began a sharp series of screams which rose and fell in intensity like waves. Ridge sat up in bed and considered the situation anxiously. Somebody was giving some woman a pretty rough time, and he wondered with a flash of apprehension if the woman might be Maria.

He sat there for a moment longer as the screams continued. They were coming more spasmodically now, as if the injured woman was entering a breathless state of agony. Binnaker was apparently questioning one of his women in the way he knew best about the escape.

Finally Ridge swung his feet off the side of the bed and reached for his pants. He had to find out if that tortured soul was Maria, and if it was, he had to do something about it He owed that woman too much, whore or not, to abandon her now.

He finished dressing hurriedly and was about to pull on his boots when he heard a faint noise outside. He drew his revolver and waited. "Parks?" Maria's voice said quietly from outside the door. "It is Maria."

Ridge pulled the door open and stepped back to let her in. She had changed out of the red satin dress back into her drab everyday costume. "I thought maybe that was you screaming," Ridge told her. "I was jus' comin' up to the big house to find out."

"The *patrón,* he hurt the Indian bitch," Maria said quietly. Though Ridge could not see her face, he could tell by the sound of her voice that she was frightened and upset by what Binnaker was doing. Though Maria had shown earlier that she had no liking for the young Indian woman who had taken her place as Binnaker's favorite, it was obvious that she had no taste for this kind of brutality. "He is drunk with the whiskey and he say Indian bitch, maybe she help Holley go. He uses the knife with fire."

She reached out to softly touch Ridge's

arm, needing the reassurance of human contact, and then as the squaw let out another agonized scream in the distance, her fingers dug sharply into his flesh. Ridge could well imagine that Maria had sampled such mindless drunken brutality from Binnaker in the past.

"It's okay, Maria," Ridge said. "You're here safe now an' I'm not going to let them hurt you that way." He shoved the door closed and then returned to the bed and sat down. "We have to sleep now, Maria," he told her. "I have to ride out with the searchers tomorrow and I need some rest. You stay here and it'll be all right."

The Mexican woman again curled up on the floor beside Ridge's cot, and he took the blanket from his bed and spread it over her. Then he took his gunbelt off again and put it by the head of the bed.

There were no more screams. The sounds of nocturnal insects and the howling of a distant coyote again dominated the night as Ridge settled back on the bunk once more.

"Cowboy?" Maria called, soft and low, from the floor beside Ridge. "You take me away. I help you, please you take me away?"

"I'll take you away, Maria," Ridge said, "and when We get to Adobe City, I'll take you to see Holley. Now go to sleep."

Ridge went to sleep thinking of the stir he would make in the Holley home when he came calling with Maria by his side. The other marshals Billy Dean worked with would be teasing him for a long while about needing a whore to save his life.

Char Binnaker's Indian squaw was clumsy with the serving of breakfast because of the thick bandages which were wrapped around the backs of her hands and arms. Both of her eyes were swollen and bruised, and one cheek was gummy with the thick poultice she had applied to the wedge-shaped burn there. Still, though, she moved with the same stoic resignation, never hurrying, rarely speaking, and never looking straight into any man's eye.

Binnaker's saloon and restaurant was crowded with grumbling, bleary-eyed men, although it was only half an hour after sunup. He and Blackie had demanded that every man in camp get up at dawn and get ready to take part in the search for the escaped marshal.

Ridge wolfed down his plate of beans and beef and was about to leave the building when Binnaker called out to him from the bar. "Parks. Come over here," he said. "Everybody's settlin' up their bills 'fore they

159

leave. Maybe for some reason or another somebody might not come back from this ride, so I want my money now." He picked up a sheet of paper from the back of the bar and glanced over it superficially, then turned to Ridge and said, "Thirty-one bucks."

Ridge gave a low whistle when he heard the exaggerated total. "Man, I shore hope I been enjoyin' it here."

"Enjoy it or not, you'll pay it or stay permanent like your pardner McDonald," Binnaker said. "An' if it cost three times as much, you'd still come back next time you was on the run an' needed a place to hide out for a while. Thirty one big ones, right now."

Ridge paid up and left, joining the other men who were at the corral saddling their horses. Mexican Joe was there with the rest of Blackie's gang, but he did not give any of those hard stares which Ridge had gotten used to receiving from him. Ridge thought Blackie must have given him a talking to last night.

Binnaker had already sent a few men out at first light to start up the back trail on foot and Blackie was taking charge of the mounted party, which consisted of about a dozen men. Binnaker was not riding along, but had discussed the expedition in detail

160

with Blackie and had given him detailed instructions about the lay of the surrounding hills and mountains and the most likely directions Holley might take. Once they were out in the mountains, Blackie planned to split the men into parties of three and four so they could comb the mountains more effectively.

President Grant was well rested and ready for some exercise when Ridge looped a rope over his neck and led him out of the corral. The rope was not really necessary because Ridge had trained the horse to obey a number of whistles and voice commands, but he did not think the others would understand him having such control over a horse which he was supposed to have stolen only a few days before.

As he waited for the last few men to get their mounts saddled and ready, Ridge glanced up the mountainside in the direction Holley had fled. About halfway up the slope, he caught a glimpse of the men who had been sent that way on foot. The group Ridge was in would take extra horses along with them, so when they linked up with the climbing party on top, everybody would have a horse to use in the search.

But despite the great numbers of men being used in this search, Ridge still had confidence that Billy Dean Holley would not be found. This was some very rugged country and much of it was not easily covered on horseback. There were many areas where a horse was a definite liability, and Ridge knew that if he was on the rim, that was the kind of place he would purposefully seek out. Tracking was nearly impossible over this rocky terrain, too, and even if some of the searchers did pick up a few signs left behind by Holley, it would not be a clear trail which could be easily followed.

At last they all mounted up and thundered away out of the valley. Blackie and Mexican Joe led the group, with the remainder of the riders forming a loose column behind. Ridge stayed back in the pack, leading one of the extra horses. He was really just along because he had no other choice, and later on, if possible, he planned to do anything he could to delay and confuse this pursuit.

It had also occurred to him that this might be the best time to try and capture Blackie Crystal and head back to Adobe City with him. Later on all the men would be in smaller groups and scattered out, and in addition they would also be out of the well-guarded valley, so it would be easier to get away with a prisoner once he had him. But that idea stayed in the back of Parkman's mind. He knew he would find out later if it was practical or not.

They rode quickly out of the guarded entrance to The Havens, then turned sharply north. Blackie led them up the long valley for a couple of miles until he found the seldom-used trail which led up into the mountains above Binnaker's sheltered valley.

The trail was narrow, steep, and twisting, and the riders were forced to string out in single file as Blackie and Mexican Joe worked out the direction ahead. They did not reach the crest of the mountain for another hour, and it was midmorning before they found the place where the foot trail up from the back of the valley reached the top.

The climbers were there and very glad to see the larger band ride up. The five men who had started out on foot were sprawled around on the ground in a small clearing. Some had their boots off and were bemoaning their sore feet, and a couple had drifted off to sleep.

As Blackie rode into the clearing and dismounted, he asked one of the men in the group, "What did you find down there? Any sign of him?"

"He come that way, all right," the man said, struggling to pull a boot on over a disintegrating wool sock. "But we knowed that 'fore we started out."

Another of the men got up and walked over to get a canteen off one of the spare horses. "He coulda gone a dozen different directions along that mountainside," he said before removing the stopper from the canteen and taking a long drink. "We didn't see no sign once we got here to the top, so your guess is as good as mine."

Blackie turned to the men who had followed him and said, "All of you stay right here in this clearing so you don't mess up no tracks nowhere 'round here. Joe, you an' Carter get down an' scout around a bit. See what you can find."

As the rest of the riders stepped to the ground and broke out canteens and tobacco, Mexican Joe and Carter moved to the edge of the clearing and started examining the rocky soil for any marks or signs which Holley might have left when he passed by there.

Ridge walked over and sat down beside one of the men who had climbed up from the valley. As he pulled his tobacco sack out of his shirt pocket and began piling tobacco onto a paper, he said, "Rough climbin' comin' up here, huh?"

"I mean to tell you," the man said, rubbing a blister about the size of a silver dollar on one side of his foot. "Them damn boots is made for ridin', not walkin', an' now my damn feet ain't goin' to be worth a tinker's dam for more'n a month."

The man was not a member of Blackie Crystal's gang and he seemed to have no interest in the project. "To tell the truth," he said, turning to Ridge and lowering his voice, "I don't really give a damn whether that damn greaser ever gets to stick his blade in no law man. I come here to hide out from the marshals, not to go trompin' 'round no mountains lookin' for one."

The man's irritation continued to mount, arid as he reached again for the hurt foot, he expanded the range of his complaints. "It ain't the same in this place as it used to was," he grumbled. "That ol' devil Binnaker, he's done got greedy an' mean as hell. Hardly any time I come here lately that I ain't seen him do a job on some poor sucker on that damn post of his. An' he loves it. I swear, I think he's crazy as a cross-eyed looney bird. He ain't never got no decent women no more either, an' even when he does get aholt of one that looks a little, better than a she-grizzly, he jus' beats 'er an' burns 'er an' scars 'er up. Crazy as hell, I think."

"Seems like he does have a right smart of

mean in 'im," Ridge agreed. "Maybe his shorts is too tight."

The man looked at Ridge, not sure whether that was a joke or he was being made fun of. But he seemed in no mood for a confrontation, so he said nothing more, nursing his sore feet in silence.

In a few minutes Joe and Carter came back to the clearing. They had made a wide circle completely around it, but found no signs of Holley.

"We don't see nothing," Joe complained bitterly to Blackie. "Maybe he go this way or that way, or maybe he turn off the trail before he reach the top. I don't know."

"Okay," Blackie said. "We'll split up an' look around." He quickly began to designate men for each group, and he put Ridge in charge of one party of four which was to work its way down the opposite mountainside toward a ragged gulch far below. Acting on the assumption that Holley had escaped on the spur of the moment without proper supplies for the trip ahead, they were concentrating their search in the direction of the nearest water supplies. Binnaker had suggested that plan before the men left that morning, and Blackie had agreed that it was the most logical thing to do.

"If anybody finds anything, fire three shots

in the air an' then leave one man at the place to direct the others," Blackie instructed. "If we don't turn up no trail by sunset, we'll meet back at the valley east of here. Tomorrow we'll look in a wider circle an' see if we can't catch him when he finally turns back in the direction of Adobe City. Okay, let's get goin'."

Ridge was disappointed that he had been chosen to lead one of the search parties. He had hoped to ride along in Blackie's group, and to perhaps find an opportunity to get Blackie away from the others and take him prisoner, but now that idea was useless.

He led his group away at a quick pace, intentionally choosing the easiest directions he could find. He doubted that Holley would stay on any rideable trails for very long, and he wanted to reduce the chances that any of the men with him would spot their quarry.

Sometime after noon, they reached the small gulch which was their immediate objective. It was a narrow fissure through solid mounds of granite, and a small stream about a foot deep and ten feet wide rushed down its middle. They paused there while the horses got a drink and the men took a break.

After some discussion with the others,

Ridge decided to head due east at an easier pace, which would bring them back out to the valley about dark. They rode steadily downward, following the course of the stream and occasionally having to leave the ravine and ride a rugged circuit around small waterfalls and other impassible stretches.

Ridge sensed that the other men were as dispirited as the outlaw he had talked to in the clearing about this prolonged search, and so he did very little to even make a pretense of looking for Holley. They had not thought to bring either food or refreshment with them, and so by late afternoon their main interests began to center around getting back to a hot meal and a drink in The Havens.

The sun had almost dropped to the peaks of the mountains west of them when Ridge led the party out into the fringes of the valley. It took about another half an hour to reach the rendezvous point.

One group was already waiting there when Ridge and his men rode up, and by dark all the others had come straggling in. No one had had any luck in finding the escaped marshal.

As they started back, one man reflected the sentiments of most of them when he said, "Why don't we jus' forget it, Blackie? Is it all that important that we find that feller an' kill 'im? There'll jus' be another to take his place."

"It jus' gripes my ass is all," Blackie grumbled. "This is really a hot shot gang I got here. Can't even hold onto one man long enough to kill 'im."

"We don't give up," Mexican Joe swore from his place beside Blackie. "We find him and bring him back so I can cut his belly open."

"We'll start again at first light," Blackie promised. "Tomorrow we'll comb the trails that point toward Adobe City 'til we flush 'im out. He's still got that wide valley to cross if he plans to head east toward town, an' once he gets out in the middle of it, there won't be no place for him to hide. We'll find him tomorrow, an' when we do get him back to camp, it won't go easy on him. Not after he's put us to all this trouble."

Ridge was as tired and hungry as the rest, and his spirits were further depressed when they rode through the pass into The Havens and he remembered that he had guard duty the next morning. Though it meant that he would not have to spend the entire next day in the saddle as he had today, it also meant that he would not be on the scene if they did happen to come across Holley. And he would also not be there to take advantage of any opportunity to catch Blackie off guard and hurry him away.

After tending to their horses, the men returned to the big house where the squaw had a hot meal prepared for them. Ridge was getting a little tired of this steady diet of meat, beans, and bread, but at least it was hot and there was always plenty, and he reminded himself that it was worlds better than a lot of things he had put in his mouth and called food before. After eating, the others settled in around drinks and coffee to talk and pass the evening, but Ridge stayed around only for a short time before going to his cabin to sleep.

Maria was not there, and Ridge guessed that Binnaker decided he had received his $20 worth. Parkman considered putting up another $20, but his money was running low and he still did not know how much longer he would be there. Besides that, Maria's usefulness and the need to have her near at hand was over, and he thought she would be just as well off back in her normal routine until the time came for him to take her out of there.

He secured the cabin and went straight to

bed. As he fell asleep, his thoughts were on a tub of water hot enough to boil eggs and steaks as big as table tops.

CHAPTER TEN

At first the faraway gunfire did not penetrate Ridge's deep slumber. The first shots were sporadic, coming in bursts of two or three at a time with stretches of silence several seconds long in between. But finally the shooting grew in regularity and seemed to slowly draw near. Then he woke.

He was on his feet with gun in hand in an instant. Then as he listened, he realized that the fight was some distance away down at the pass. Elatedly he dressed, strapped on his gunbelt, and picked up his rifle.

Outside a few men were standing near the doorways of their cabins, some wearing only their longhandles or pants, but all carrying rifles and sixguns. They were staring down toward the pass, and as Ridge looked in that direction, he saw the bright spears of light coming from the rifles of the guards high up on the cliffs. The staccato of the shooting from the cliffs and from the pass below sounded like the rattle of gravel on a tin roof.

"What in the hell's goin' on down there?" Nate Teller, a member of Blackie's gang, grumbled sleepily from the doorway of the neighboring cabin.

"Dunno," Cy Wynn answered from where he was standing about fifteen feet away. "Must be somebody tryin' to get in or out."

"Yeah, but listen to all that shootin'," Teller said. "Sounds like an army down there."

It was an army, Ridge knew. The U.S. Army, and probably as many marshals, sheriff's deputies, and Adobe City policemen as Henry Lott could manage to round up. For now, they were being stalled by the three guards in the rocks above, but with as many men as Lott probably had with him, that should not be a problem for too long. In this darkness, the rifles of the guards would not be as effective as if it was daylight, and it would also be difficult for them to detect anyone who began climbing up through the rocks toward them.

As Ridge stood and watched, the number of flashing guns in the cliffs grew from three to four, then six, and soon it was impossible to tell how many men were up there as members of Lott's raiding party scaled the

173

heights to take care of the outlaw guards. Soon the shooting died down and then stopped.

Ridge hurried away then, knowing he did not have much time before Lott's forces regrouped and attacked the buildings within the valley. He wanted to find Blackie Crystal and stay near him so there would be no chance of his escaping in the confusion. He was trotting past the big house toward Blackie's cabin when Char Binnaker stepped out onto the porch. He was barefooted and wore only his trousers, with his suspenders pulled up crookedly over the shoulders of his grimy long johns. He held a revolver in one hand and a rifle in the other. "You! Parks!" he shouted at Ridge. "Get your ass in here an' pick a window."

Ridge stopped and turned to face Binnaker. "I was goin' down to check with Blackie," he said, hoping to escape the assignment he had been given.

"To hell with Blackie," Binnaker stormed. "I want some good shots here in my house when they storm it, an' we ain't got no time to waste arguin'. Blackie'll prob'ly end up here anyway."

Ridge hesitated an instant. He considered just shooting Binnaker and going on, but by that time there were too many men racing around in all directions nearby to take the risk of not being seen. Reluctantly he mounted the steps and entered the building, walking over to stand in front of one window so he could look out. Binnaker was still outside shouting at men to come in and defend his house.

In a minute Maria came into the big front room, her arms loaded with rifles and boxes of ammunition. A lamp had been lit and set on the bar, but it was turned down low and the woman did not see Ridge near the front of the room until he spoke to her. "Maria," he said. "I been wonderin' where you were an' if you was all right."

"Parks!" she said elatedly as she dumped her load on a table and rushed over to him. She threw her arms around him and he patted her back reassuringly. Finally she looked up at Ridge, her face betraying the fear and apprehension which she felt. "We die now maybe, huh, cowboy?"

"Naw, Maria, I don't think so," he told her. "Here's what I want you to do right now so you'll be safe. Go out the back way an' hide in the rocks down by the shack where they had Holley. Get way up against the wall of the cliff, an' lay down flat on the ground. Stay there 'til I come for you. It may be some time before this is over, but you stay there. Okay?"

"Binnaker, he tell me to stay here. He say carry the guns and bullets, make food," Maria said worriedly.

"Jus' don't worry 'bout what Binnaker said," Ridge told her. "In a minute things'll be crackin' 'round here so fast, he won't know where anybody is or what they're doin'."

"The army kill us all," Maria sobbed. "They kill my cowboy."

"Listen, Maria," Ridge said, deciding to take a chance to relieve some of her fears. "Those are my friends down there. They're marshals an' army men, an' they know I'm in here. They're not goin' to kill either one of us. Now jus' do what I said. Get goin'!"

"Okay, I go," Maria turned and hurried back through the doorway into the kitchen.

Ridge turned to look back out the window in front, but in a moment he heard a violent argument in Spanish back behind him in the kitchen. The screaming voices of two women continued for a moment, then there was a violent crash and all was quiet again. Ridge went over to the doorway, his gun drawn, and looked into the kitchen.

Another of Binnaker's Mexican women was sprawled out in the middle of the floor. She was unconscious and bleeding slightly from a fresh gash across the middle of her forehead, and a large glass mixing bowl lay shattered in a hundred pieces around her. But Maria was gone. Ridge chuckled to himself and returned to his window in the front room.

Binnaker had disappeared somewhere out front, but in a minute two more men he had sent came in to take positions on the ground floor of the building. Later three more men came in and went upstairs. At last Binnaker himself returned, closing the big front door behind him and dropping the stout crosspiece in place across it.

"We got food an' water in here to last a helluva long siege," he told the three men in the front room. "We're gonna hold this place 'til they either give up an' leave, or we find some good way to escape outa here. You all got that?" Ridge and the others mumbled their agreement and then Binnaker lumbered upstairs.

"Who in the hell are they out there, anyway?" one of the men in the room asked as he crashed out a pane of glass with the butt of his rifle. Ridge glanced over at him and recognized him as a man which the others merely called by the nickname "Swabbie."

"Marshals, maybe" the other man there

answered. He was either named or nick-named Tooter. Ridge did not know which. "Or the army. It was bound to happen to this place sooner or later. The Havens was just too good to be true."

"That's just wonderful as hell," Swabbie exclaimed. "The army an' the marshals come chargin' in here an' ol' man Binnaker starts talkin' 'bout how maybe they'll give up an' go away, or 'lowin' as how maybe we'll all escape. Guess he thinks we could jus' climb that damn rock face back there with our horses on our backs, an' then jus' ride the hell away from here." He paused and glanced worriedly out the window for a moment, then continued with his gripes. "I don't see why they had to pick right now to come in an' clean this place out anyhow. 'Nother couple of days, I'd been gone. Hell, I was lightin' out Thursday for Nevada."

"That's tough," Tooter mumbled sarcastically. Ridge could tell his mind was too much on the fight ahead to be interested in listening to Swabbie's bellyaching.

In the distance Ridge began to hear the pounding of many horses' hooves. He and the other men moved to a side window and looked out. "Oh, hell," one of the men said as he smashed a couple of panes of glass out of the window so he could get a better look. "We're in for it now."

In the gray light of earliest dawn, Ridge saw as many as thirty or forty men spread out in a ragged line charging at a full gallop toward the row of buildings from the east. About half of them wore the blue uniforms of the U.S. Cavalry and the others were dressed in ordinary clothes. As they drew nearer, the sound of gunfire started up from the roof and the upper stories of the building they were in, and the attackers answered quickly with a withering barrage.

All three of the men moved back to the windows at the front of the building, and in an instant the whole area was plunged into a pandemonium of gunfire and death. Clouds of gunsmoke filled the room and fogged the air outside, and even after it became impossible to see any of the attackers in the thin morning light, the two men in the room continued to fire their weapons randomly and desperately out the windows. Ridge took only an occasional pot shot, keeping his fire well over the heads of the men outside. An incredible amount of gunfire was pouring out of the building at the exposed horsemen, and though Lott had brought in a superior force of men, they were suffering a lot more casualties than they were inflicting. It was soon evident that the momentum of their charge was broken and that they would have to retreat or face annihilation.

On some unseen signal, the riders began falling back, taking shelter behind a long, high hummock about 200 yards away. Most of the men immediately dismounted and flattened themselves out along the crest of the small rise while a few others drove the horses farther away to safety.

"By damn, we drove 'em back!" Swabbie shouted with excitement. "I think I got me one of the bastards, too. Just laid my sights right on his belly button an' knocked him slap out of the saddle. Did you see it, Tooter?"

Tooter did not answer. Ridge glanced over to where the third man had been and saw him lying in a twisted heap along the front wall. His eyes were open wide in a blank, dead stare and his mouth was gaping. His throat was a gory, bloody mess.

Swabbie spotted the dead man at the same instant and muttered, "Would you look at that! They plumb done a job on ol' Tooter. They shore did."

"Nailed him square in the gullet," Ridge agreed. "Too bad for him."

"Yeah, too bad," Swabbie said without much remorse. "He was an okay feller, I guess. Didn't know him too well myself."

"Me neither," Ridge said, turning his attention back outside. Though there was a momentary lull in the action while the attackers retreated, when they took their new positions, the shooting started again almost immediately. A pane of glass above Ridge's head shattered suddenly, showering him with broken fragments, and he ducked down quickly behind the thick log walls. Outside shots were returned from up and down the row of cabins, some at the hummock in the distance and some into the bodies of the six or eight unfortunate attackers who lay dead and dying in the clearing in front of the buildings.

Lott and his men had their work cut out for them now. The outlaws had shown their willingness to fight instead of giving up, and the way they were scattered out, they would have to be routed out of almost every cabin individually.

And Ridge had still not figured out a way to deal with his specific problem. He had no idea where Blackie Crystal and Mexican Joe were, and even if he did, it now seemed too late to get to them. The attackers out there would not know him from the others, and he would be an open target if he strayed outside the building.

The potshots continued for the next half hour or so as morning slowly made its appearance in the eastern sky. Finally, during a lull in the shooting, a call came from across the broad clearing in front of the big house. "Surrender yourselves to the law!" It was the deep, commanding voice of Captain Henry Lott. "There's no chance of any of you getting out of here alive if you don't give up."

Char Binnaker answered back with an obscenity and levered out several shots from his rifle.

"We've got a field piece down in the pass," Lott said. "We'll turn those buildings into kindling."

"You try it," Binnaker taunted. Ridge decided he must be behind the fortifications on the roof of the building. "I got a buffalo gun up here that says I can turn any man into a corpse who tries to lob a cannon ball at me." He fired several more quick rounds and there was a scream of pain out among Lott's men.

Binnaker had himself a good location up on the roof of the two-story building. Just a couple of riflemen could do devastating damage to any number of men who tried to charge the building, and from his vantage point, he could probably also reach any cannon crew that tried to bring a field piece in and aim it at the stronghold. Binnaker was not a stupid man, and he had planned the location of his buildings with just such an eventuality as this in mind.

But Ridge knew that Lott was bound to have a few tricks of his own prepared. It was not really a matter of whether the soldiers and marshals could overrun The Havens and capture the outlaws there, but more a question of how long it would take and what cost it would require in lives. But Lott apparently did not want to make another costly charge on the buildings. He had the advantage, both in men and position, and he could more afford to wait than the outlaws could.

An hour passed with only occasional shots being fired back and forth. The day arrived, clear, bright, and warm as both forces waited tensely for something to happen, some deed or event which would trigger a sudden change in the standoff. It was a particularly tense time for Parkman, who was caught in the midst of his enemies with his friends out there shooting at him. He fired an occasional shot, always high, for the benefit of the man there with him, but his main concern was staying down and making sure he was not hit by a random shot from Lott's forces.

The stalemate finally ended when Binnaker began blasting away with renewed fury up on the roof. After a moment he paused long enough to bellow out, "Look out, boys! They're comin' down from the top!"

Telling the other man in the front room to stay where he was, Ridge dashed through the kitchen and out onto the back porch. He saw about a dozen men rappelling down the side of the steep cliff behind the big house and line of cabins. As he watched, Binnaker's bullets connected with a couple of climbers, who went limp and fell swiftly to their deaths.

By then shots were cracking in all directions again, but Ridge still risked stepping out from under the cover of the porch to see if he could get Binnaker in his sights and silence his deadly rifle. He saw two rifle barrels extending out beyond the wall of the barricade, but he saw nothing of the men up there.

He went back in the building and through to the front room. Swabbie was firing steadily out the front windows. Since his concentration was focused on the soldiers and marshals outside, it was easy for Ridge to walk up behind him and unceremoniously pop him across the back of his head with his rifle butt.

Then Ridge grabbed Swabbie by the collar and drug him through the kitchen and out the back door. Keeping low and running as he pulled his burden along, he covered about 50 feet before dropping the unconscious man on the ground. Then he raced back into the big house. On his second trip out, he carried the Mexican woman Maria had fought with when she was leaving. Ridge dropped her by the unconscious body of Swabbie, then returned to the building.

In the kitchen he found a large can of lamp oil which he carried into the front room. In a minute he had the floors and walls saturated with the oil and he moved into the kitchen to do the same there. Finally he stepped out onto the back porch and fished in his pockets for a match.

By then some of the soldiers had succeeded in reaching the ground, and one who hid behind a clump of rocks a couple of hundred feet away began snapping off shots at Ridge. One shot thunked into a post near Ridge, and another tugged at the sleeve of his shirt as he ducked back inside the building.

Back in the front room once again, Ridge found a can of matches on the shelves of supplies Binnaker stocked. He picked up a chair and threw it through a side window, then quickly leaped out and hunkered down beside the building.

Bullets were flying everywhere and the battle had become totally chaotic, but Ridge ignored the gunfire as he struggled to light the matches and pitch them over his head through the window. When they kept going out, he finally tore a thin strip of cloth from his shirt and bound a bundle of about a dozen matches together. He struck the bundle on a rock, pitched it over his head into the room, and waited. In a moment, he began smelling the smoke and seeing flames.

The next move was the most risky he had attempted so far. Staying bent over low, he raced out into the open toward the nearest of the cabins. Bullets whizzed all around him and one caught the heel of his boot and brought him down, but he rolled on his left shoulder and came back to his feet, still running.

When he reached the cabin, he dived through the side window without slowing up. One outlaw was in the building and he spun around quickly, but he recognized Ridge before he shot. It was Lettershaw, one of the members of Blackie's gang. Curled up on the center of the room like a sleeping child was Carter, another gang member. His face was gone and a large pool of blood around his head was slowly soaking into the hard dirt floor.

Ridge rose to his feet, bruised and stiff, and looked back out the window he had just come through. The entire bottom floor of the big house was a mass of flames which were licking out the windows and quickly working their way upward. As he watched, the flames found a stock of ammunition somewhere and an explosion roared out, shattering what windows had not already been broken, and spreading the fire even faster.

"Bullet hit a lamp over there," Ridge explained to Lettershaw breathlessly. "I had to get out of there." Lettershaw didn't answer. He was busy pumping rounds out the front window.

"Where's Blackie?" Ridge asked hurriedly.

Lettershaw turned away from the window with his back to the front wall and began reloading. "Two cabins down, if he ain't dead yet," he said without looking up. "But there ain't no use you tryin' to go down there. He's in the same jam we are, an' you'd never make it anyway."

Not bothering to answer, Ridge crossed the room and flung open the shutters of the window on that side. The rest of the cabins were only about ten feet apart, and he spotted a small depression behind the next one which would provide some cover.

Lettershaw was watching him now, his brow wrinkled in a scowl, so Ridge did not bother to try to knock him out or shoot him. He just leaped out the window and raced over to dive in the ditch he had spotted. He crawled along on his belly behind the cabin, then stood up and raced over to dive in the window of the cabin Blackie was supposed to be in.

But the cabin was empty. Blackie was gone.

It took Ridge several more minutes to work his way to the rear of the last cabin. From inside it he could hear a couple of men still pumping shots out at the attackers, but the hottest of the fighting seemed to be centered around the big house and the cabins on the other side.

Ridge turned back and looked at the big house. The flames were well up into the second floor by then, and Ridge watched a woman with her skirts on fire leap from a second-floor window, roll off the porch roof, and start running in terror across the clearing in front of the building. A bullet from somewhere ended her agony.

But on the roof of the building, in defiance of the flames, Binnaker and another man were still pouring out a devastating amount of gunfire. Then the second man suddenly threw down his rifle, leaped from behind the barricade, and began running across the roof with his hands held high. Binnaker shot him in the back before he could jump to the ground.

But all that was behind Ridge now. No more than a dozen of the outlaws were probably alive by then, and though they were still putting up a desperate fight, Lott and the troops could handle them. He had to think about Blackie now. Where was he? Had he survived the gun battle and somehow slipped through the tight ring of soldiers and marshals?

Ridge remembered Blackie's account of how he and a few others had escaped when they were attacked by the Rangers in Mexico, and he guessed that the situation was probably the same here. A clever criminal like Blackie Crystal would almost always have escape options ready when the fire got too hot. He was not the sort to make a desperate stand and fight it out to the death. More than likely he had taken the first opportunity to run away.

And in this case, Ridge figured, his flight

was most likely up the secluded back trail into the mountains. Seeing how completely Billy Dean Holley had eluded fifteen or twenty armed and experienced searchers, Blackie had probably figured he could do the same and completely lose himself in the countless square miles of mountain wilderness which surrounded them.

But Ridge vowed that that was not going to happen this time. He would get Blackie and take him back, no matter what it took or how far he had to go.

He rose and sprinted toward the jumble of rocks along the cliff's base behind the tack shed. He knew if he could make it that far, he could work his way around the rim of the valley under fairly good cover to the beginning of the trail. It would be slow going, but it was the only way, and probably Blackie would have to take the same tedious route.

He made it about halfway to the rocks before the shots began peppering around him. Then finally one connected. The bullet glanced off the action of the rifle he carried, then dug a deep furrow up his left forearm. He ran on, dropping the ruined weapon as he leaped for the shelter of the rocks ahead.

This was the place he had told Maria to wait for him, but she was not in sight. He called out as loudly as he dared, thinking that she might have found some better hiding place nearby, but still she did not appear. There were footprints in the dust there, the heavy imprints of worn boots.

By then the blood was gushing from the wound to his arm and the pain was startling. He cut away the left sleeve of his shirt and saw that the wound was a ragged furrow about eight inches long and half an inch wide. The bullet, which had spent itself in his flesh, was lodged just under the surface of his skin near his elbow.

With his sheath knife, he probed around gingerly until he had removed the bullet, and then he quickly cut off the right sleeve of his shirt. He wrapped it tightly around the wound, and though the doth was immediately soaked with blood, he thought it would be a good enough bandage for a while.

Cautiously he began working his way through the rocks toward the trail. It was slow going, and in some places he was forced to lie down flat and crawl forward to stay out of the line of fire of Lott's forces.

The roar of another explosion made Ridge stop and turn back toward the battle he had left behind. The noise had apparently come from somewhere inside the inferno of Binnaker's burning building, and to Ridge's surprise and amazement he spotted Char Binnaker still behind his fortifications on the roof. But he was on fire now, waving his arms in mortal agony and almost seeming to be going through the gyrations of some sort of ritualistic death dance as he perished.

Then suddenly the whole brilliantly flaming structure trembled on its foundations and started to collapse. It fell inward, as if hell was sucking it into the earth, and the eerie form of Binnaker disappeared amid the clouds of sparks and flames which rushed aloft.

As for away as he was, Ridge could still feel the heat of the fire, and the nearest cabins on each side of the inferno had both begun to burn.

It was a fitting end for such a sadistic, evil man, Ridge thought. In the manner of his death, Char Binnaker had received a foretaste of his eternity. When he first set the fire, Ridge had not intended that Binnaker or anybody else should die in it. He only knew that he had to find some way to silence the guns of the men in the rooftop stronghold if the attack was ever to be completed. But he felt no guilt over the outcome of his deed. If ever there was a man who deserved to die, and die horribly, it must be Char Binnaker.

Within a few more minutes he neared the entrance to the trail up into the mountains. The battle was far away now, and the volume of shooting had decreased considerably as the last few remaining outlaws were either killed or gave up. Ridge risked stepping out into the open long enough to examine the ground near the trail.

There were fresh tracks there heading up the mountainside. He drew his pistol as he started into the rocks and up the trail. From the heights above, it might be possible for Blackie to see him slipping through the rocks in this direction and he did not want to walk into a trap. He climbed slowly, preferring stealth to speed.

When he had made it about a quarter of the way to the top, he began to hear the low sound of voices ahead. He paused for a moment and listened, then began to move forward cautiously. The voices stopped in a moment, but he knew about where they had been. When he was within about 30 feet of the place, he stopped to listen again.

There was a soft low noise ahead, like a gentle cooing or moaning. He took a few more silent steps, and then as he rounded a large rock, he spotted a man's legs ahead. When he got nearer, he saw that it was a dead Indian. He wore a white man's boots and trousers, but his shirt was buckskin and around his neck was a soldier's yellow neckerchief. A battered blue cavalry hat lay nearby. The Indian was shot in the shoulder, stomach, and neck, and he was quite dead.

Then he heard the quiet voice again, quite close this time. "Poor Holley. You don't die, okay?"

Ridge passed the dead bodies of a soldier and a member of Blackie's gang before he reached the place where Maria and Billy Holley were. When Maria looked up and saw Ridge, her face was a portrait of despair.

Billy Holley, his head cradled in Maria's lap, had an ugly bullet wound on the left side of his chest. His drawn face was deathly pale under his deep tan, and his eyes were closed.

"Is he dead, Maria?" Ridge asked as he kneeled by the woman.

"No. He is alive still."

Holley opened his eyes then and looked up at Ridge vaguely. He tried for a grin as he said, "Can you believe this shit? I got shot."

"I can see that, pardner," Ridge said quietly. "Jus' take it easy."

"After all them days dawn there, I finally get away an' . . ." He paused to cough and

194

the spittle which trickled down over his lip was pink with blood. ". . . An' then I come back down here an' get my fool self shot."

"What did you come back for?" Ridge asked.

"The Army scouts, those two down there," Billy said, nodding his head toward the men below him on the trail. "I run into them before daybreak this mornin'. They said they was tryin' to find some back way down into the valley. I told them 'bout this place an' said I'd lead them down."

He paused to cough again and Maria carefully wiped away the blood with a corner of her skirt. Then he went on. "We was right at the top when the shootin' started, an' we started down in a hurry 'cause we wanted to be in on the fight. Me 'specially.

"It was probably my fault we got jumped, what with the way I was tearin' down this trail like a danged empty-headed greenhorn. There was jus' three of 'em, but they hid behind the rocks an' jus' blasted the hell out of us when we got here. It was Blackie an' some Mexican an' that other one down there. The Indian got him."

"So there's jus' two of 'em now?" Ridge asked.

"Blackie an' the Mex."

"So what are you doin' here, Maria?"

195

Ridge thought to ask finally.

"I see Blackie go and I follow him," she said. "I follow him for you."

"Wal," Ridge said. "Guess it's a good thing you did. Now what I want you to do is start back down the trail. Circle around so you can get to the soldiers an' tell 'em Billy's up here hurt."

"I go," she said, easing Billy's head off her lap before leaping to her feet and racing away.

"She'll have some help up here soon," Ridge reassured Holley as he began tearing the young man's shirt away. The wound was an ugly, blue-black hole, thumb-sized where it went in at the base of his ribs, and about the size of a pipe bowl where it came out the back. Blood was oozing out both holes with a slow, steady pulse.

" 'Bout all I can do right now is plug this up," Ridge told him as he tore the shirt up for bandages. "But I'm goin' after Blackie an' maybe I'll bring his ears back to you like the bullfighters do."

"Jus' get 'im, Ridge," Holley said weakly. "That's one mean sonofabitch. Jus' take him out, an' don't be too careful how you do it."

"He's as good as hung." Ridge made two thick square bandages and plastered them over the open wounds, then used several longer strips of the shirt to tie them into place. When he was finished, he wiped his bloody hands on his pants and quickly rolled a cigarette for Billy. He lit the cigarette and put it in the young man's mouth, then said, "That's all I can do for now, pardner, but help should be here soon. Jus' hold on. I done took too many chances gettin' you loose to have you go an' die on me now."

"Get 'im, Ridge," Billy repeated, and then he closed his eyes. Parkman stood up, retrieved a discarded rifle from nearby, and started away.

CHAPTER ELEVEN

Ridge believed he had gained some time on the two fleeing outlaws. Setting up the attack on Billy Holley and the two scouts had taken awhile, and now he believed they were no more than half an hour ahead of him. He thought for the first time that the chase might not necessarily be a long one, and that was a good thing.

Although he considered the bullet crease up his arm only a minor hindrance at the moment, he knew that over a prolonged time it could become a serious problem. In this climate, an untended wound began to fester quickly, and Ridge had known of men losing arms and legs, and occasionally their lives, from wounds less serious than his.

He had seen wounds cauterized with the blade of a knife heated red hot in a fire, and he had even used that method once himself on the leg of a friend who had been badly clawed by a bobcat in an area where no medical help was available, but he also knew that it was extremely painful and did not always work. Sometimes the burn from the hot knife became as badly infected as the bullet wound would have.

Henry Lott had probably brought a doctor along on the raid, or at least there would be a medic among the troops in the valley, but Ridge did not want to abandon his chase and go back down to seek medical help, not with Blackie and Joe so close up ahead. So for the time being, he just tried to forget about the heavy throbbing ache in his left arm as he continued his climb up the mountain. If the chase stretched out over a long period of time, he would give more thought to the injury later.

But soon after leaving Billy, Ridge discovered something encouraging. He found that he had a blood trail to follow.

There was plenty of blood in the little clearing around where Billy lay, but it had not occurred to him there that some of it might belong to Blackie Crystal or Mexican Joe. But no more than 30 feet from where Billy lay, Ridge spotted the first few drops spattered along the side of the trail where one of the hunted men had apparently stopped for a moment.

Ridge stooped and probed one of the

penny-sized splotches with a finger. It was still fresh, about the consistency of thick grease, which confirmed his suspicion that he was not far behind the two outlaws.

Every few feet on up the trail, he found another drop or two of blood, and in one place he found a moist red handprint on the side of a large boulder. Somebody was hurt bad. One of the two fleeing men, weakened from losing so much blood and unable to climb any farther up the steep trail, was going to have to stop soon and make a stand. Ridge only hoped that when that happened, the second uninjured man would feel no loyalty to his companion and would go on alone. He stood a much better chance of taking the two men if he faced them one by one.

About midway up the trail he found a place where a wad of cloth, saturated with thick dark blood, had been thrown aside. It appeared to be a piece of the heavy, home-spun material that Mexican Joe Rodriguez's shirt was made of. Ridge nodded his head thoughtfully, knowing it could not be much longer.

He moved on up the trail very cautiously now, knowing that he could not be absolutely quiet but still trying to make a minimum of noise on the loose gravel underfoot.

He reached a place in the trail where it was so steep that he had to scramble up on his hands and knees, grabbing at the available rocks and scrub brush ahead to pull himself up. His head and shoulders finally topped the crest of the grade and he was looking cautiously over the more level stretch ahead when the gun went off. Its sound was muffled but still close by, and the bullet went searing by dangerously close to his head.

He let go his handholds and went sliding quickly back down the trail on his chest, stopping after about ten feet. With his pistol ready, he gazed upward for a moment, trying to recall everything he had seen in that brief glimpse he had. He had not seen where the shot came from, but it had been somewhere slightly to the left of the trail, and the noise was odd somehow, altered by wherever the gunman had chosen to hide.

He turned to his left and began climbing slowly up an almost sheer rock face at the side of the trail. The man up ahead had chosen a perfect place to stop and wait and Ridge knew his only chance of going on was to circle around somehow and discover where the man was hiding.

He scaled up the stone wall for about 15 feet, fighting the pain in his rebellious left arm with sheer willpower. Then he cut back to the right until he neared the area where the gunman had fired on him. But as he crawled cautiously across the top of a large flat rock and peered down at the small open area, he saw no one. He waited. If one or both of the men was down there, probably they would tire of the prolonged silence and eventually ease over to peer down the steep trail to see if Ridge was lying below, wounded or dead.

A few minutes passed, and then he heard a low bitter curse muttered in Spanish. It seemed to come from directly below him. Quietly Ridge eased forward until he could peer down over the edge of the rock he was on, and there below him were the telltale smears of blood on the ground.

The lower portion of the rock was about a foot off the ground, leaving a deep crevice large enough for a man to crawl back into. Wounded and probably knowing he would soon die, Mexican Joe had reacted with animal instinct, wedging himself far up under the shelter of the rock like a wounded creature seeking to hide its body from the carrion scavengers. There was no sign of Blackie anywhere around, and Ridge was sure the bandit chief must have abandoned his dying companion and gone on alone.

Ridge heard a low growl of agony from deep under the rock, and then more Spanish, which seemed to be a curious mix of prayers and obscenities.

"Give it up, Joe," Ridge said from atop the rock, "or you're a dead man."

"Then I take you to hell with me," Joe hissed out at him.

"Come on out an' do it, then," Ridge said. He began slowly easing his way along the top of the rock toward one edge. "I'm jus' sittin' here waitin' for you to try it." When Joe did not answer, Ridge went on. "No, come to think of it, I guess you like it better under there. Lizards an' snakes always hide under big rocks, don't they?"

The Mexican began another string of bitter oaths in his native tongue.

"You know, Joe," Ridge continued. "I sure got a laugh when I made such a fool out of you by lettin' that prisoner go. An' then when I backed you down about it, I really enjoyed that. I'd give up a month of my marshal's pay to see that expression on your ugly face again."

Silently Ridge eased to the ground beside the rock, staying back beyond Joe's line of vision. He heard a low scraping sound begin under the rock.

Then suddenly the Mexican rolled out

from under the rock into the open, his speed belying the severity of his wound. He stopped, lying flat on his back, and fired his pistol wildly upward toward where Ridge had been. Ridge fired once. His bullet entered the bottom of Joe's jaw and penetrated his brain, killing him instantly.

Ridge crossed the clearing and paused a moment to stare down at his victim. Even in death, Mexican Joe Rodriguez's face was set into that same twisted snarl which Ridge had grown so accustomed to seeing, and hating, when he was alive. He stepped over the dead outlaw and started on up the trail.

Blackie Crystal, not far ahead up the mountainside, would be doubly on his guard now after hearing all that shooting, but Ridge decided to gamble that the outlaw chief would not stop and set up an ambush. He would have no way of knowing how many men were pursuing him and his thoughts would most likely be only on reaching the top of the mountain and disappearing in one of the several directions available to him. Parkman moved forward as quickly as the steep trail and his own waning strength permitted.

Finally, no more than 100 yards from the crest, Ridge stopped at last to catch his breath. He looked upward and caught one quick glimpse of Blackie's dark form moving among the rocks at the head of the trail. There, at the very brink of freedom, Blackie paused and looked back. His eyes locked with Ridge's, and though the distance was great, Ridge thought he saw the outlaw grinning back at him in triumph. Ridge lifted his rifle to his shoulder and snapped off a shot, but Blackie was gone from sight before the report of the weapon faded away across the mountainside. Ridge sucked in a couple more deep breaths and hurried on.

When he was almost to the spot where he had seen Blackie, Ridge heard one quick shot some distance away to the right. He paused, thinking that maybe the outlaw had run into some of Lott's men on top of the mountain, but when he heard no more shooting, he hurried on, rushing across the fairly flat surface of the mountain crest with a desperate burst of energy.

He soon found the reason for the lone shot. Rounding a jumble of rocks, he saw a dead horse lying on the ground, a single bullet hole in the side of its head. Ridge realized then that the two scouts who found Billy Holley must have left their horses here when they decided to follow Billy down the trail into the valley. Blackie had come upon the horses, taken one, and killed the other so Ridge could not use it to ride after him.

Ridge began running at full speed then, following the clear trail of hoofprints which Blackie's stolen horse was leaving. In a minute, as he burst into the open, he spotted Blackie far away, urging the horse down the side of the mountain along the same trail Ridge had taken when he led the group of men in search of Billy Holley the day before. Ridge ran on ahead a few more yards, then stopped beside a rock about the height of his shoulders. He leaned his rifle against the side of the rock, took careful aim, and squeezed off a shot.

It was too far for a Winchester to throw a bullet with any accuracy, but Ridge had to take the chance because it was his last one. Even rested and uninjured, he would stand no chance of catching Blackie on foot, and if the bandit succeeded in getting out into the boundless wilderness ahead, no amount of soldiers or trackers would ever catch up with him again.

The tiny distant form of horse and rider moved on for a fraction of a second longer, and then the horse stumbled and teetered sideways. Finally man and animal disappeared from view as they tumbled into a deep gorge on one side of the trail.

Suddenly Ridge found himself leaning

against the big rock for support, his cheek still nestled against the stock of the rifle as it had been when he shot. He felt a dizzy, light-headed sensation which swirled through his head like thick, befuddling clouds. It was caused by the loss of blood, he knew, as well as by the exertion of his last frenzied burst of speed.

In a moment the feeling passed and he stood back up straight, staring down for a moment at the ledge of rock where Blackie had disappeared. There was no movement down there, and instinctively Ridge knew there would be none. Finally he started down toward the place, but he no longer hurried.

He reached the spot where the horse had been when he fired the shot, and gazed down into the ragged trough beside it. The gorge dropped away at a sharp angle for about 50 feet, its sides coated with loose shale and ragged outcroppings of rock.

At the bottom lay the dead horse, its head twisted at an awkward angle back in Ridge's direction and its legs splayed out unnaturally. On the far side of the carcass lay Blackie Crystal, both legs pinned under the body of the animal.

"You still alive down there, Crystal?" Ridge called out. He did not want to expend the energy it would take to descend the gorge unless Blackie was still among the living. If the outlaw was dead, the soldiers could come around and retrieve his body later.

There was a weak movement below, and finally, slowly, Blackie raised his head up to look in Ridge's direction. His features were contorted with agony, but it seemed that Ridge could still detect a spark of hatred burning in the outlaw's eyes.

With obvious difficulty, Blackie raised a pistol up and fired it randomly in Ridge direction. The shot hit more than 20 feet to Parkman's left. Ridge raised his rifle calmly to his shoulder and fired one shot. With an echoing retort the pistol exploded in Blackie's hand.

Char Binnaker's big log house had burned down to nothing more than a large pile of glowing embers which popped and protested only occasionally as the last of the timber was consumed, but several of the other cabins were roaring infernos. Only a few minutes before the commander of the Army troops had sent several of his men out to start fires in the remaining buildings which had not been set ablaze during the battle with the outlaws.

Ridge Parkman sat under a large canvas lean-to which had been hastily thrown up by the soldiers as an improvised field hospital. As he watched the cabins burn, he smoked cigarettes and took an occasional swig from the canteen of water one of the soldiers had given him.

Under the canvas roof more than a dozen men, soldiers, deputy marshals, and outlaws lay on pallets on the ground, waiting for the one Army doctor to get around to tending to their wounds. Ridge himself had been there for nearly two hours, but he was one of the least seriously wounded men and was content to wait and be treated last.

On the ground outside were two long rows of bodies laid out in an orderly formation, military style, each covered with a drab green blanket. One row, the longest, was the soldiers, marshals, and others who had died, and the second row was the outlaws who had been killed. It had been a bloody day in The Havens. The final toll from the fighting was somewhere between twenty-five and thirty, but it was impossible to get an accurate count since several bodies had been consumed by the fires in the big house and the cabins on either side of it.

Beyond where the bodies lay were the five captured outlaws who had been uninjured.

They sat despondently in the dust, their hands tied together, while three soldiers with fixed bayonets on their rifles guarded them with seething anger, seeming almost to hope that one would try to escape.

Half a dozen soldiers who had started up the trail half an hour after Ridge had found him on the top, wandering listlessly around, and had brought him back down to the field hospital in the valley. While two troopers brought Ridge down, the rest had set about to gather up all the bodies scattered up and down the mountainside. That was more than two hours earlier.

Billy Dean Holley lay now near Ridge, unconscious from the sedative the doctor had given him before beginning the job of dressing and closing the wound. Ridge had been surprised and delighted by the news that his young friend would probably pull through. Before, when he saw the way Billy had looked up there on the mountain, grayishly pale and spitting up blood, Ridge had not held out much hope. Since Billy had been attended by the doctor, Maria had been there with him most of the time, but had left a few minutes before to get some food for Ridge and herself from the army field kitchen.

From somewhere toward the direction of

the burning cabins, Henry Lott stepped under the canvas shelter and came over to Ridge. His face was streaked with dirt and sweat and he looked exhausted, but he had been one of the lucky ones in the fight and was uninjured. As he knelt beside Ridge he said, "Well, by damn, it was costly as hell but we did it, didn't we? We finally cleaned this hellhole out once and for all."

"Yeah, it was a good job, Henry," Ridge said, "but I shore am glad it's over."

"You did some fine work here, Ridge," the captain said. "In all that shootin' I'd about given you an' Holley both up for dead, an' then when that fire started, I commenced to wonderin' if we'd ever even find your bodies to know what happened to you. It was mighty fine news when that woman come up an' said you was both over there on the back side up that hidden trail."

"I set the fire myself," Ridge told Lott. "I figgered ol' Char was jus' doin' too much damage up on the roof with that damn repeater of his, an' there wasn't no other way to get 'im down. I didn't partic'ly mean for him to burn up, but I can't say I'm too sorry about it. He was a bad hombre, jus' mad dog mean. Have you found his bone yard yet?"

"One of the men come across it awhile

211

ago," Lott said. "Ain't no way of tellin' how many bodies he dumped out there over the years, the way the wolves got the bones so scattered out, but the man that found it said he counted twenty-seven skulls."

"Binnaker loves killin', 'specially in slow painful ways. 'Fore we leave here somebody's got to chop that pole over there down or burn it or somethin'. That's where he done a lot of it."

"It'll come down," Lott promised. "When we ride out of this place, there won't be one stone lyin' on top of another. We're even settin' charges, an' when we leave, we're goin' to blast the pass closed. Then there won't be no more Havens, ever again."

Their conversation was interrupted by an agonized scream from the doctor's operating table at the other end of the tent. Both Ridge and Lott looked down in that direction and the captain said, "That'll be Crystal. They jus' got him down from the top awhile ago."

Only a few minutes before, Ridge had learned that, miraculously, Blackie Crystal had survived even the revolver blowing up in his face. After the final shot, Ridge had just assumed that the outlaw was dead, but the soldiers combing the mountaintop had found him still alive. But the job of getting

212

him down was difficult and time-consuming. Crystal had been in such bad shape that the men who had brought him down had been forced to build a sort of travois which they used to carry him down the side of the mountain.

"Is he gonna make it?" Ridge asked Lott.

"Prob'ly so, if he don't die of shock from everything the doc plans to cut off. One leg's comin' off at the knee, an there wasn't much left of his right hand an' forearm but a nub. His head was a mess, too. Looked like somebody give him both barrels from about five feet away."

"The last shot I fired at him hit his sixgun an' it blew up on 'im."

"Well, he won't have much time to worry 'bout bein' a cripple. The circuit judge is holdin' court open back in Adobe City waitin' for us to get back, an' I already got some nooses tied up an' waitin' to be used. It'll be a fine day. A good day for the law."

"I got the names of the four that killed Mark Franklin," Ridge said. "I don't see but two of 'em still alive, Stone an' Wynn out there, but maybe the others are in here somewhere shot up. We can check later."

"That's good, real good," Lott said with satisfaction. "I reckon we've got hangin' charges on jus' about every man here, but with them four it'll be an extra special pleasure."

Ridge gazed out at the row of bodies, the subdued prisoners, and the flames and smoldering embers of the buildings beyond, wondering that just a few hours before this had been one of the most secure and legendary bandit strongholds in the West.

"We did it up right, didn't we, Henry?" he said with a tired but pleased smile. "We fixed 'em for Mark Franklin."

"Yeah. For Mark Franklin," Lott agreed.

CHAPTER TWELVE

Ridge Parkman sat at the small table in his hotel room tightening the last screw on his Colt revolver. He had been there for the last half hour, giving both the pistol and his rifle a thorough cleaning and oiling. When he was finished, he checked the gun over, spinning the cylinder a couple of times and testing the action of the hammer and trigger. Finally he reloaded the weapon and slid it into his holster, then pulled the rawhide loop down over the hammer to keep it in place.

On the bed behind him lay his saddlebags, already packed, and he had sent word down to the boy in the livery stable to have President Grant saddled and ready for the trail. He had been in Adobe City for the past nine days, spending most of his time in the courtroom and witness waiting rooms, but orders had just come in for him yesterday and he was heading back to Denver now for a new assignment.

It was the quickest series of trials Ridge could ever remember attending. The nine prisoners who had been brought bade from The Havens had been tried in three separate proceedings. First came the murder trial of the three surviving members of Blackie Crystal's gang who had hung Mark Franklin after the Adobe City robbery. That took two days.

Next Blackie and the same three gang members were tried for the bank robbery and the murder of several civilians and policemen in Adobe City. That was the longest trial, taking four days to hear the testimony of all the local residents and bank employees who had been witnesses to the crime.

And, finally, a two-day session was held to determine the fate of the five remaining outlaws who had been a part of the defense of The Havens when it was attacked.

Ridge Parkman had been a key witness in all three trials, and he had sat through the entire eight days of court sessions, sweating in the packed courtroom with what seemed like half of the local population who took time out from their pursuits to watch the proceedings. The local sheriff had made an effort to randomly select impartial jurors who would hear the evidence without bias and make their decisions fairly, but the weight of the evidence was overwhelmingly against all nine men. To a man, they had been condemned to hang.

Ridge could still remember the sight of Blackie Crystal and the remnants of his gang lined up in front of the judge to be sentenced. Blackie, less a couple of parts of his body and still bandaged extensively, on the judge's instructions, had been helped to his one good leg to hear his doom decreed. The judge had passed the sentence without hesitation, and had even told Blackie Crystal sternly that he felt it was a shame that wanton killers of his sort could only be executed once. The crowd had burst into a frenzy of cheering and applause at that, and it had taken every law man in the room to keep them away from the prisoners.

The day of the executions had been set for the day after tomorrow, and already people from the outlying regions were beginning to gather in town to see it. There was talk that the Central and Pacific would begin running extra trains starting the next day to accommodate all the extra passengers from as far away as Denver who were coming for the event. Seldom, even in the wildest of western towns, were nine men all hung on the same gallows on the same day, and what had only a few days before been a local attitude of bitterness and grim hatred toward the outlaw prisoners had since the sentencing turned into almost a carnival atmosphere. Local hotels, restaurants, saloons, and other businesses were doing an even better business than during the last burst of gold fever some years before, and the gallows being constructed in a large clearing near the courthouse had become almost a local tourist attraction.

But Ridge was leaving before the big event. He did not like the crowds, and the sideshow aura which was quickly taking over in town made him nervous. He wanted Blackie and the others dead, had wanted it ever since that day some time before when he had to cut Mark Franklin's decaying body down from a tree, but he felt no desire to stay around and watch their deaths. He could see no pleasure to be derived from it.

As he was rolling up his gun-cleaning gear and stowing it in its place in the saddlebags, there was a low knock on the door and then it opened.

Maria stepped into the room, carrying a bundle of folded towels in one hand and a pail of water and scrub brush in the other. Though the cotton print dress she wore was simple and plain, it was clean and well cared for, as was the rest of her. She had a bright, cheery smile on her face, but as she looked around the room and saw that he was packed to go, her smile faded.

"Cowboy, you go away now?" she asked, setting the pail on the floor and dropping the brush and towels on the bed.

"I'm headed back to Denver," Ridge confirmed. "That's my home, or at least it's as near as a feller like me gets to havin' a home. I'm goin' back for a new assignment."

"You come back to Adobe City sometime?" she asked in a voice heavy with sadness and apprehension. She was close to crying and Ridge went over and put his arm around her shoulder.

"Hell, Maria, I'm in an' out of this place all the time," he said. "An' from now on, every time I come here, I'll come to see you an' I'll stay in this hotel."

"Good. You come back," Maria said, smiling despite her brimming eyes. "I stay here. I stay work for *Señor* Gobels."

"That's right," Ridge instructed her. "You keep this job an' you stay here. It's a good place for you." When the large party of soldiers, law men, and prisoners had returned from the raid on The Havens, Ridge had told Henry Lott about the help Maria had provided and how Billy was alive because of this Mexican woman. Lott had called in a favor from Hubert Gobels, owner of this hotel, and had secured a maid's job here for Maria. At first the elderly German proprietor had only taken her on reluctantly and Ridge had worried that she might not be able to keep the job for long, but then Gobel's attitude had begun to change remarkably and he had warmed up to her rather suddenly.

Still standing with his arm around Maria, Ridge told her quietly, "Maybe you'll never have to go back to the kind of life you had before. If you ever have any trouble, you tell Henry Lott or Billy Holley an' they'll let me know. But ol' man Gobels seems like a good enough sort an' I think he'll take care of you all right."

"*Señor* Gobels like Maria very much. I take care of him, too," Maria said. Her dark eyes twinkled with a look of mischief which was impossible to misinterpret.

Ridge laughed out loud as he realized suddenly the reason for the elderly hotelkeeper's abrupt change of heart toward his new employee. "You hussy, you," he chuckled, giving her a familiar slap on the rear.

Maria gave him a parting kiss and a long

hug. With her head resting on his shoulder, she muttered one final regret. "Damn war."

Ridge moved bade from her so he could look down at her face. He was still on the verge of laughter, but he knew that if that lie he had told Maria about a war wound ever got out to the other marshals in the area, he would quickly quit seeing much humor in it. "That's just our secret," he reminded her. "About the damn war an' all. Okay?"

"Okay, cowboy. Maybe someday you get better, eh?"

"Maybe," Ridge smiled.

When he left the hotel and walked down the street to the livery barn, the boy had President Grant out front waiting for him. As Ridge mounted up, the boy said, "Have a good trip, marshal."

"Thanks, son," Ridge told him. He turned the horse and started to ride away, then stopped and turned back to the youth. "Say, I almost forgot somethin' didn't I? A promise I made awhile back."

"Oh, it's okay," the boy said self-consciously. "Marshal Lott, he paid for stablin' your horse for you."

Reaching deep into the pocket of his trousers, Ridge said, "I'm a man of my word. I keep my promises." He pulled out two silver dollars and flipped them one by one into the air. The boy deftly caught them, his face beaming with delight.

Ridge had seen Henry Lott for the last time earlier that morning, so he had only one more stop to make before he left for Denver.

He rode halfway up Missouri Street, then turned down a small lane beside the Holley house, and left his horse tied in their tiny back yard. Rosalie, who had been working in the kitchen in the rear of the house, saw Ridge through a window and came out to meet him on the back porch. Her hair was pulled back on her head and tied with a ribbon for housework, and it seemed to Ridge that she looked particularly fresh and pretty this morning.

Her glance did not miss the fact that he had his horse with him on this visit, nor did she overlook the bedroll and packed saddle-bags tied behind the saddle. But her greeting gave no hint of the feelings she might be having about his departure. "Hi, Ridge," she said with a smile. "I think Billy's asleep, but I just put on a fresh pot of coffee. Come on in and have a cup with me."

"That sounds good," Ridge said as he mounted the two board steps and followed her into the house. He took a seat at the small kitchen table while Rosalie poured two cups of the steaming black coffee and brought them to the table.

"How's your patient today?" Ridge asked her as she sat down across the table from him.

"He must be a lot better," she said. "He's getting ornery and hard to control. He wanted to get up today, and it took mother and me both to convince him to stay in bed. The doctor said he should not be up moving around for at least another week."

"I figgered he wouldn't tolerate lyin' flat on his back for too long, bullet hole or no," Ridge commented. "I know how he feels, 'bout them doctor's orders. The doc told me I should keep this arm in a sling for a week, but I jus' couldn't stand that blamed thing hanging down there, pullin' my head over like a hangdog pup. I wore the sling all the way back to the hotel, an' then I threw it out the window."

"You men!" Rosalie said with mock reproach. "It's a wonder any of you survive, always riding around the mountains getting shot up and beat up."

"It's a livin' I s'pose," Ridge grinned. It had been that way between them since he got back. They had spent several evenings together both here at the house and out around town, but after the initial expressions of gratitude were over, they had kept their talk light, indulging in a lot of banter and avoiding more serious topics like the future and what place they might have in each other's lives.

But now there was an odd, subsurface tension between them. His horse was saddled and waiting outside, and Rosalie knew without being told that the closeness they had shared in the past few days must necessarily be a passing thing.

Several times over the last week Ridge had felt that he must be a madman for even considering leaving Adobe City and Rosalie. In this beautiful young woman across the table from him was the stuff that men fought for and died for. He could feel the old hungers pulling at him, and he knew that years from now, as he sat beside some desolate mountain campfire, fighting the cold and the lonely stirrings within him, he would still berate himself for letting this woman pass out of his life.

But his course was set. He was a man of action and movement, a man who was willing to take on the hardest jobs and get them done because he had no ties, no loved ones anywhere to make him cautious, and sometimes perhaps even afraid. That might all change someday. He might eventually reach a point when he was ready for it to change . . . but not yet.

After their little joke, an odd moment of silence fell over them. Rosalie stared down at her coffee cup, stirring it idly, and Ridge found himself gazing out through a back window to where his horse was tied to the flimsy picket fence out back.

"Mother's gone shopping," Rosalie said finally. "Billy's appetite is improving and so we decided to fix a big meal tonight. I wish you could stay and join us."

"Me, too," Ridge said. "But they want me back in Denver. I wired I'd be along as soon as the trials were finished."

Rosalie looked up at him then, her head cocked slightly to one side, her eyes gazing directly into his. There was a certain question in her look. She was trying to fathom why he would not stay here and see if things worked out between them. But she did not understand it at all, Ridge knew. He could scarcely understand it himself, why he had to go out and mount up in a few minutes, or why he had to leave Adobe City.

From somewhere in the back of the house, Billy Holley called out, "Mama? Rosalie? Will somebody bring me a glass of water?"

Rosalie rose and went through the other

rooms of the house to where Billy was. Ridge heard them talking quietly back there for a moment, and then Rosalie came back into the kitchen.

As she got a glass of water from the bucket on the kitchen counter, she told Ridge. "I told him you were here and he said come on back. He's feeling good this morning. Here, you can carry the water to him." Ridge admired the way she had quickly sloughed off the moody tension of a moment before. She was not going to try to use any feminine wiles on him or lay any burden of guilt on him for his decision, and he appreciated that.

Despite the encouraging descriptions Rosalie had given about Billy Dean's improvement, he was still pale and thin, and his eyes had not yet completely lost that sunken look Ridge had seen when he first found the young man tied up in The Havens. He was lying in the middle of a large soft bed, covered over with a multitude of blankets which had been lovingly tucked in around the edges by one of his two attentive nurses.

"I jus' stopped by one last time 'fore I headed out," Ridge said, pulling a straight-backed wooden chair over beside the bed and sitting down. "Your sister says she thinks maybe you'll live a couple more days yet."

"Yeah, I feel lots better," Billy confirmed. "I'm itchin' to get up out of this bed, but them two mother hens out there won't let me lift a muscle without makin' a federal crime out of it."

"There's time, ol' hoss," Ridge advised. "Ain't no use rippin' out stitches an' messin' yourself up again jus' 'cause you're bullheaded an' want to show how tough you are."

"Naw, it's more than that, Ridge," Billy glanced past him to make sure his sister was not hovering nearby, and then went on in a lower tone. "It's a lot of little things. You ever had to sit back while a woman give you a bath, I mean a woman in your family? Or have you ever had to take a leak while your ma or your sister held the pan? I'm tellin' you, it's downright embarrassin'."

Ridge laughed out loud at that. "Ol' Bed Pan Bill," he chuckled. "Scourge of the Rockies."

Billy gave Ridge a wry look and said, "It ain't really all that funny, Parkman. You try it sometime."

Ridge stopped laughing then and changed the subject. "Have you given much thought to what you'll do when you get back on your feet? You stayin' with the marshals?"

Billy looked up, suddenly worried, and asked, "They still want me, don't they? Has Henry said anything?"

"Jus' that he's needin' you back astride a horse an' out in the field. But I thought that maybe . . . you know, sometimes when a man gets all shot up, he figgers maybe he's learned his lesson an' gets out. None of us hold it against him if that's the way it turns out to be."

"I'm a marshal, Ridge," Billy said firmly. "You been shot before, but you still got your badge, don't you?"

"Yeah, I think so," Ridge said. He patted his pockets, then decided it must be somewhere in his saddlebags. "I still got it somewhere."

"I still got mine, too, an' I plan to keep it 'til somebody says I can't wear it no more."

"I'm glad, Billy. We need your kind to sort of balance things out with all the Blackies an' Binnakers that's still around."

They talked for a few more minutes before Ridge decided it was time to go. He rose from the chair and reached out to shake Billy's hand before leaving. "So take care, ol' son, an' I'll be seein' you someplace on down the trail."

"I'll do it, Ridge, an' you do the same."

When Ridge got back to the kitchen, Rosalie followed him out the back door and over to where President Grant was tied and waiting. Before mounting, he turned and found Rosalie standing quite close to him. She reached out and took his hand, then said, "In a way, I still wish you had let me make that promise to you."

"It's been on my mind, too," Ridge told her. "Every time I smelled that perfume you wear, I kept thinkin' as how maybe I did deserve some special kind of reward for bringin' Billy back. But you jus' keep the thought, an' maybe we'll both see how we feel next time I pass through these parts."

"I won't wait for you, Ridge," Rosalie said quietly with a tinge of sadness in her voice. "I'm not foolish enough to do a thing like that. If the right man were to come along tomorrow . . . But it's like you said. Maybe next time you're through here, we'll see what's changed and what has not."

Ridge put his hands on her waist and pulled her to him for a kiss. They stayed together like that for a moment, then slowly parted. As Ridge put a foot in the stirrup and stepped astride President Grant, Rosalie turned away and started back to the house.